The Oregon Trail ™

hmhbooks.com

The text was set in Garamond.
The display text was set in Pixel-Western, Press Start 2P, and Slim Thin Pixelettes.
Illustrations by Gustavo Viselner

Library of Congress Cataloging-in-Publication Data is on file.

ISBN: 978-1-328-62714-8 paper over board
ISBN: 978-1-328-62715-5 paperback

Printed in the United States of America
DOC 10 9 8 7 6 5 4 3 2 1
4500751508

The Oregon Trail™

THE WAGON TRAIN TREK

by
JESSE WILEY

Houghton Mifflin Harcourt
BOSTON   NEW YORK

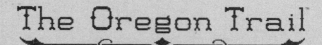

The Oregon Trail

GO WEST, Young Pioneer

It's 1855, and you and your family are headed west to Oregon City to start a new life. Your pa is a doctor—and the leader of your wagon train. You're getting older now, so it's your responsibility to help Pa and Ma, along with your two Newfoundland dogs. You will lead your team of six wagons from

Independence, Missouri, all the way to Oregon City. Pa is eager to join a new practice there, and you're excited for a new home, wide open spaces, and the journey ahead.

But it won't be easy. Your trek is fraught with many dangers. Bad weather, dishonest people, and disease are just a few challenges that can end your trip on the Trail. As the wagon-train captains, it's your job to make sure that everyone gets to Oregon City safely. The folks in your wagon train might not always agree, so you'll also need to be the mediators and carefully settle any disputes.  Choose carefully, listen to others, and make wise decisions. Above all, keep your wagon train together.

Only one path will get you safely to Oregon City. There are twenty-three possible endings full of danger, surprises, and adventure.

You have to cross a dangerous river; how do you do it?

You're surrounded by howling coyotes; what do you do?

Your wagon train is at odds; will you split up?

Your decisions along the way might send you somewhere unexpected or put you at odds with other pioneers. Or, even worse—you might not make it!

Before you start, be sure to read the Guide to the Trail on page 168. It will prepare you to make wiser choices.

At some points along the Trail, you'll get advice from guides, people from various Native American Nations like the Kansa, the Cayuse, and the Klickitat; from members of your wagon train; or from Ma and Pa. At other times, you'll have to trust yourself to make the right decisions. Choose wrong, and you'll never make it to Oregon City!

It's up to you!
What will you choose?

→ Ready? ←

LET'S BLAZE A TRAIL TO

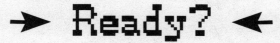

OREGON CITY!

Gardner Junction
APRIL 27, 1855

Rise and shine!"

You roll over and groan. It's just before dawn at Gardner Junction, where the Oregon Trail and Santa Fe Trail split off. Pa and Ma have already risen with the other wagon-train families. They are feeding the oxen and preparing a hot breakfast over the campfire.

It's been nearly fifty miles since you, Pa, Ma, and your two Newfoundland dogs, George Washington and King George III, left Independence, Missouri. It was the last major settlement before starting on the Oregon Trail. Pa is a doctor who has received an invitation to help start a practice out in Oregon City. Doctors are desperately needed in the West, and your family couldn't pass up the opportunity. Not only is he the doctor caring for your entire wagon train, but he's also the leader. There are six wagons in total—one man, Mr. Mason, is a banker with *two* wagons. Your family owns one, and the other three wagons belong to the Whittakers, the O'Neils, and the Joneses. As

the wagon-train leaders, your family is responsible for making sure everyone gets to Oregon City safely.

So far you've crossed over pleasant open prairie and gentle hills, but the Trail will only get more difficult from here. The stopping points and trading posts are few and far between, so you must ration your food and plan your travel route carefully. The land will become rockier and more treacherous, and sudden storms could wipe out your entire wagon train in an instant. Accidents are common on the Trail, as well as sickness and even death.

You've already been walking nearly eighteen miles a day since leaving Independence, but you'd like nothing more than to roll back over and sleep just a few more minutes.

"Hurry up before breakfast has come and gone!" Pa flips the bacon. "Up and at 'em. Slugabed didn't even hear the morning bugle!"

You hear the sizzle of bacon. The delicious smell wafts into your tent.

One of your dogs starts whining. Pa laughs. "All right, you scoundrel, you'll get your food in a minute."

You can't let your dogs get to the food before you! You quickly dress, put away your bedroll, and clamber out of your tent.

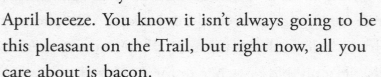

The grass is soft and green beneath your feet, and bunches of sunny yellow wildflowers sway in the cool April breeze. You know it isn't always going to be this pleasant on the Trail, but right now, all you care about is bacon.

King George III and George Washington bound up to you, covering you with slobbering licks. You laugh and push them away.

"I'm awake, I'm awake!" You take a seat next to Pa and help him pour cups of coffee for everyone.

Ma enters your small camp, pulling your dairy cow behind her. "Don't let those dogs near that food! There's plenty of rabbits about."

"Did Trixie wander off *again?*" You take a bite of bacon. "That blasted cow!"

Ma nods, tying Trixie carefully to the back of the wagon. "We need to make sure she's always tied up during the night. I don't know how she got free. Don't we have dogs to herd her back in?" She shoots a dry look to both the Georges. They just wag their tails. "Hmph! No tasty bacon for you lazy hounds."

King George plops to the ground with a huff.

You slip the massive, shaggy dogs each half a bacon strip anyway. Their tails wag gratefully.

"Your ma's right, though." Pa wipes morning dew from his spectacles. "Food will get precious up ahead on the Trail. We have to make sure we conserve our supplies and plan out exactly what we should ration."

You have just over six hundred pounds of food on the wagon—two hundred for each person—and you'll need to restock at trading posts and hunt where you can.

As you sink your teeth into a warm hunk of bread, you grimace at the thought of going months without a big slice of Ma's famous apple pie. Your mouth waters at the thought of dessert. You didn't realize how many things you'd miss until these past few days, but you know that adventure and opportunity lie ahead in Oregon City!

As the sun rises over the flat horizon, you help Pa and Ma clean up from breakfast and prepare for the day's long travel ahead. As the only child, it's your responsibility to help feed and care for the animals, cook, and clean. You also keep a journal of your time on the Trail. You finish your entry from yesterday, which unfortunately isn't that exciting.

Mrs. Whittaker approaches your campsite. "Dr. Howard, Mrs. Howard, good morning." Her husband, Mr. Whittaker, is a skilled carpenter and is expected to be instrumental in fixing broken axles and repairing damaged wheels on the Trail. They have three children: Annie and Matthew, who are about your age, and a baby named William. Annie and Matthew have daily chores like you, but they also have a horse and some livestock. They get to take turns riding on horseback to herd loose livestock, including your own cow, Trixie, who always wanders off. You wish you had a horse, too. After only a few days of walking, your legs already ache.

"Good morning, Mrs. Whittaker." Ma grabs the coffee kettle. "Care for some?"

Mrs. Whittaker shakes her head. "No, thank you. I'm sorry to disturb you, but I know we need to start moving soon, and . . . I wonder if you've heard the rumors going around?"

Pa frowns and glances at Ma. "What rumors?" Ma shakes her head.

"There's a bad bout of cholera up ahead on the Trail." Mrs. Whittaker points. "A few families want to try for the Santa Fe Trail instead."

Pa adjusts his spectacles. "That sounds a bit hasty. We should ask someone who knows the Oregon Trail better than we do. I'm sure we can find a guide among the other wagon trains here before they leave."

Mrs. Whittaker puts her hands on her hips. "Do you really want to risk it?"

Pa and Ma look at each other, then turn to you.

"You're old enough to help make this kind of decision. What do *you* think we should do?"

If you want ask a local Oregon Trail guide about potential sickness ahead, turn to page **31**

If you want split up and go on the Santa Fe Trail, turn to page **69**

You're old enough to help your parents make important decisions along the Trail—why not make this one too? You glance over at Ma. She's still deep in conversation with the two Kansa women. You learn their names are Tajé Mi and Ke Wák'o.

"You've got yourself a deal." You shake the fur trader's hand and he thrusts three blankets at you. Before you know it, all your spending money is gone—and so is the fur trader. He disappears out a side door in a blink of an eye.

You try to ignore the funny smell emanating from the blankets and rush up to Ma. "Look what I got! Now we'll be sure to stay warm in the mountains."

Ma frowns. "Where did you get those from?"

"A fur trader. He just left."

"That man with the fur hat?" You nod and she shakes her head. "Oh, dear."

"That man is a crook." Tajé Mi points to the door.

"There is a warrant out for his arrest. Soldiers outside have been looking for him."

You stare down at the blankets. "What should I do with these?"

"Throw them away." Tajé Mi looks to Ke Wák'o. "They are likely not good blankets."

You don't want to tell Ma that you spent all your money on these. When you and Ma head back to the corral, you sneak them into the back of your wagon.

You use the blankets that night and discover that they are threadbare and ratty. You're cold so you use one of them anyway.

You wake up in the morning with small bites all over your body. The blankets are infested with bugs! You feel queasy and your head hurts.

Within the next few days, you burn up with a fever. You have chills, stomach pain, and a rash. Deadly tick fever has set in.

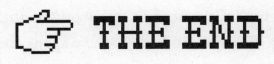

You and the other families are split over what to do. To keep the peace, you tell Pa that going downhill and avoiding Devil's Backbone might be the better option.

"It might give the oxen a chance to rest for a little while." Pa wipes his hands on his kerchief. "All right. We'll head downhill from here."

Mr. and Mrs. Mason are relieved. Their oxen were tired out after the slog through the river, and they've already lost so many supplies.

After you and Pa gather large rocks to weigh down the wagons, you help the oxen gradually make their way down the steep descent of the rocky terrain. Then, you hear a shout. One of the wagons has tipped over.

Pa and the others rush to help, leaving you to hold the oxen steady on the sharp incline. They manage to right the wagon.

"Before we go on, we need to throw out anything we don't need." Pa wipes his brow. "The wagons are too top-heavy. It's too risky."

Mr. Mason turns purple. But Pa and the others are in agreement. Even you and Ma must throw out household items and a few gardening tools.

"Hopefully someone will come along and find a use for them." Ma looks at the objects scattered along the Trail.

You give her hand a squeeze. "I'm sure they will."

That evening, when you've corralled your wagon train, you hear the sound of hoofbeats. Five men on mangy horses enter your camp. They say they're a group of fur traders.

"We're just passing through." Their leader smiles a toothless grin. "Nice wagons ya got there."

"Thank you." Pa tips his hat. "Good luck with your hunting, gentleman."

You don't like the way they eye your wagons. They look more like a group of desperate bandits than fur traders. After they've passed your campsite, you tell Pa and Ma your concerns.

"I don't trust them either." Ma turns to Pa. "We met some fur traders back in Independence. These men seemed very different."

"Well, what do you think we should do?" Pa's brow is furrowed.

"Maybe we can keep a special watch tonight." Ma paces by the fire. "What do you think?"

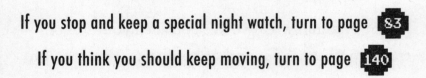

If you stop and keep a special night watch, turn to page **83**

If you think you should keep moving, turn to page **140**

You should try to get help." You look up and see the worsening weather. Maybe if Ma leaves now, before the snow gets too deep, she'll be able to blaze a trail to Fort Boise and bring back a group of people on horseback.

The wind howls and lashes thick snow against your tent. You huddle under blankets, trembling. A sudden ache settles into the pit of your stomach. You fight back a wave of nausea. *It's just nerves. Nothing more.*

Ma's hands are on her hips. "I don't like the thought of leaving you here on your own . . . Especially when your pa's not looking so well . . ."

"I'll take care of him, Ma." You pull up the blanket. "You should go now before the storm gets worse."

Ma wraps a thick scarf around her neck and puts on Pa's jacket. "Try to keep the campfire going and keep giving him water—only water that's been fully boiled. I'll be back as soon as I can." She disappears through the flaps of the tent.

Hours pass. Pa shakes uncontrollably—and it only gets worse. But he's not the only one. You begin to feel so weak, you can hardly move, much less keep the campfire going.

You collapse as darkness sinks over you. Your wagon train trek ends here.

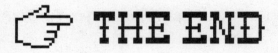 **THE END**

You decide that there's nothing for you in Big Springs. Pa still has a job offer in Oregon City, so you keep moving forward. Other families don't agree. The Whittakers decide to head back to Big Springs to get work there.

You're sad to see Annie and Matthew go, but you have to focus on hunting. You have no money left for food. Soon, you and Pa are out on the plains hunting for jackrabbits and antelope. The Masons and the Joneses team up and look for berries in the brush. You see something move in the grass a distance away. Pa is busy looking for larger game, so you hurry over to see what it is. But it's not a rabbit.

It's a rattlesnake! You hear the hiss and rattle of its tail as it sizes you up.

You're frozen, not sure what to do. But you see that it's curled up right next to a dead jackrabbit. A rabbit whose fur you could sell and whose meat could feed your family tonight. But snakebites can be deadly. You probably should run away.

But you desperately want that rabbit.

You pick up a rock and throw it at the snake. You miss, and it hisses, lashing out toward you. You jump back, and your ankle is stuck in a prairie dog hole. You let out a cry.

But the next second, a new pain sinks into your leg. The snake bit you! Dizzy, you try to shout for Pa, but it's too late. Your journey ends here.

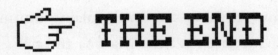 **THE END**

You've already delayed in Fort Hall long enough. You and your family start off for California right away. You've stocked up on food and additional supplies. It makes no sense to backtrack to Salt Lake City.

You've asked around and have settled on traveling to Sacramento, where Pa hopes to open his own practice. The journey won't be easy. Heading south means that you'll be going through mostly desert terrain. Instead of preparing for the snowstorms and frostbite you'd face in Blue Mountain territory, your struggle on the California Trail will be mainly finding sources of water and game to hunt.

The Whittakers and the O'Neils insist on stopping in Salt Lake City. You scratch King George's head as you listen to Pa and Ma argue with the other families, but it's no use. The others split off to form their own wagon train.

You're alone on the California Trail.

Pa sighs. "We might have just made a mistake."

"It's too late to worry about that now," Ma tugs the wagon reins.

Soon, you see nothing but craggy hills, low brush, and white sand. There are no trees in sight. No animals aside from the occasional lizard or snake slithering through the underbrush.

But, most important, you travel miles without seeing one critical resource: water.

You stop to check the map, but you realize that you forgot to purchase one of the California Trail. The map you have is useless.

You keep moving, but soon your water reserves run dry. The oxen bray, barely slogging through the hot sun. Your mouth feels like it's stuffed with cotton. Your shoes are filled with pebbles and sand.

You think you see water ahead, but it's always just out of your reach.

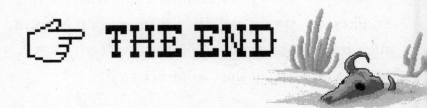 THE END

You and your parents agree that while you'd hoped to make it to California, Salt Lake City is a fine place to settle down. Plus, Pa has already begun to establish a reputation as a great local physician.

"It'd be foolish to keep going when we've already begun to start something here." Pa squeezes your hand.

"I'd rather not have to travel all those miles through the desert." Ma smiles at you, relieved.

"I don't know," you joke, "sounds like fun to me."

You all laugh. But soon you find that your wagon train is upset that you've stayed so long. Mr. Whittaker tells your pa that they're going on with or without you.

"Looks like we're going to have to say goodbye to the rest of our wagon train." Pa sighs. "Unless they want to settle down here with us."

But the remaining two families choose to keep going to California. They leave soon after. You catch word from passersby that there was a severe drought and the Whittaker wagon train didn't make it. You knew that splitting up was never a good idea.

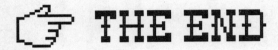 **THE END**

We should ask a local trail guide," you suggest.
You've made it this far, after all. And who knows if
the Santa Fe Trail is any safer?

Pa nods. "I agree. I can't let the practice in
Oregon City down, not when I've already agreed to
join."

Mrs. Whittaker hesitates. "Well . . . if you think
it best, Dr. Howard, we'll wait to hear what this guide
says."

"Good choice, Mrs. Whittaker," says Ma.
"Splitting up the wagon train is not a great idea.
We're safer if we stay together."

You and Pa venture off to find a trail guide amid
the other wagon trains gathered in the area. There are
so many families traveling along the Oregon Trail!
Some wagons are overstuffed with items—so full they
look like they might burst. You recall what someone
in Independence told Pa and Ma: not to overfill your
wagon with valuables, because you'd probably end up
tossing most of them away, anyway. Many pioneers
shipped valuable items around South America and up

past California to Oregon City. Your family had to ship your ma's precious grand piano in a huge boat, hoping it will meet you there.

Finally, you come across a man named Captain Carter. He tells you that there *is* a concern for sickness ahead.

"I'd take a different route." Carter chews on a blade of grass. "Cross at the Wakarusa River and head on up to Big Springs, past Mount Oread. Some folk avoid the Wakarusa crossing, as there's no ferry

yet, but take it slow, and the going might lower yer chances of running into trouble with the sickness. And make sure yer food is cooked, and yer water fully boiled 'fore you drink."

"Of course. Thank you." Pa shakes the captain's hand before you head back to your own wagon train.

The morning sun blazes in the sky as you start off toward the Wakarusa River Crossing. Ma and Pa take turns sitting in the driver's seat, holding the reins of your team of oxen, while you walk alongside. Your wagon is too full for you to sit, unfortunately. But it's such a nice day that you don't mind walking. King George and George Washington bound beside the oxen, chasing after prairie dogs and jackrabbits that scurry across the plains. Soon, you've been walking for hours. Ma and Pa start humming a pleasant song, and Pa tosses you a piece of dried jerky to chew on.

"I wish we had a dog!"

You turn to see Annie Whittaker trotting up beside your wagon on their horse. She's got a big straw hat on to block out the late-afternoon sun. You haven't spent much time with the other children in the wagon train, but you're excited to make new friends.

"I wish we had a horse." You kick some dirt. "All we have is a wandering cow named Trixie."

Annie grins. "We've had to corral her back in once or twice already, haven't we?"

You both laugh. Annie's brother Matthew comes running up to join in on the conversation. George Washington barks and leaps over to him, covering him with licks.

"Careful, or you'll drown in their drool." You smile and pull your dog down.

Matthew laughs and pets George Washington's head. "Hey, look!" He points past you. "The Wakarusa River!"

You turn and see a thick grove of trees that dip

down sharply among patches of limestone rock. Then, you hear the sound of rushing water.

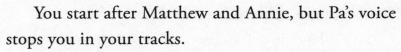

"Let's go see it!" Matthew races off.

You start after Matthew and Annie, but Pa's voice stops you in your tracks.

"Wait! We're stopping here to unhitch the oxen to let them feed before crossing. Don't run off—you'll make them nervous."

But Annie and Matthew are already bounding away down toward the river. You want to prove that you're just as brave and adventurous as they are. Should you follow them?

If you wait until Pa has unhitched the oxen, turn to page **155**

If you run after Annie and Matthew, turn to page **43**

I'm so hungry." You stare longingly at the general store in Big Springs' town square. Your mouth waters at the thought of biscuits and gravy and fresh jelly cake. But you lost most of your money in the river. You had eight hundred dollars leaving Independence. Now you have only two hundred.

"We'll have to sell off two of our oxen to get more food and winter supplies," says Pa grimly. "We can still make it with the two remaining oxen, but we'll need to save as much money as possible. We don't have much to trade."

You glance back at your damaged wagon and see Mr. Whittaker storming over to your family. Behind him, Annie and Matthew watch sadly from afar. They lost their beloved horse trying to climb Devil's Backbone.

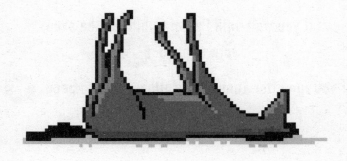

"This is all your fault," Mr. Whittaker snaps at Pa. "We should never have trusted you as our leader. We've lost nearly everything. It was our dream to get to Oregon City. Now we'll have to go back to Independence until we can find a way to pay for the damage *your* leadership caused."

Before anyone can respond, he stalks away.

Pa sells off two more oxen and your dairy cow, Trixie, to get a few hundred more pounds of food and several new sets of clothing, including a new pair of shoes for you. Now you have only two oxen left.

After you've rested for two days in Big Springs, your family continues on alone. Both the Whittakers and the Masons have gone back to Independence.

But with only a third of your original oxen team still intact, your daily pace is a slow crawl.

One night, only a few days after you've left Big Springs, you notice one of the oxen lying down.

Pa looks him over, but the animal won't get up. "He's sick. We need to rest until he's better."

The next day, the ox dies. Soon after, your last ox gets the same illness. Your dreams of trailblazing to Oregon City end here.

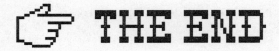 **THE END**

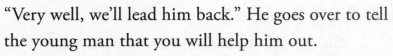

He's been through enough, Pa," you say. "Let's help him get back to the fort."

"I'm sure the others will understand." Ma looks at Pa. "We'll lose time, but it's the right thing to do."

Pa scratches his beard. "Very well, we'll lead him back." He goes over to tell the young man that you will help him out.

"What's going on?" Annie and Matthew come up beside you. She's riding their horse today, with Matthew looking especially glum about it.

"We're going to help that man get back to Fort Boise."

She grimaces. "Pa and Ma won't like that."

The Whittakers aren't pleased with the idea of traveling all the way back in the opposite direction. The Masons aren't either.

Mr. Whittaker steps onto your camp. "Someone at the fort was telling us that the snowstorms are going to get very bad this time of year. I don't think we should tarry here, much less backtrack to Fort Boise."

Pa just shakes his head. "I'm a doctor, Mr. Whittaker. I have to do what I know to be right. In this case, it's helping this young man."

"Let's simply help him bury his family, provide him with a map, and keep moving." Mr. Whittaker puts his hands together. "Please, Doctor. We don't have time or resources."

Pa and Mr. Whittaker argue for several minutes before Mr. Whittaker storms off. Pa sighs. He tries to enlist the help of the other men to dig graves before you return to Fort Boise. No one is happy with the idea of turning around. Everyone is also petrified of contracting the deadly cholera.

While the men dig graves and bury the bodies, they tell Pa that they want to keep moving on the Trail.

"We'll continue on the Trail. You can catch up to us, Doc." Mr. O'Neil leans on his shovel.

But your parents don't like this plan, and neither do you. The wagon train is safer traveling together.

Alarm fills your camp when the young man you're helping doubles over in the grass. Ma and Pa rush to help him. He is shivering and burning up with a fever.

"He has cholera too." Pa touches his forehead. "Everyone stay back."

"We'll do more than that." Mrs. Mason and her husband don't wait for the rest of the wagon train— they leave within the next several minutes. You see the second of their two wagons trailing off into the distant mountains.

The other families stay for the time being but hover in a corral some yards away. You and Ma help Pa to bring the young man blankets and water, but you're afraid it might be too late.

"What if we hurry him back to the fort, Pa?" you suggest. "Before he gets worse? Maybe you can treat him better there?"

Pa nods thoughtfully, his brow creased with

worry. "Good idea, but on the other hand, it might be too late by then. We don't want to risk it."

Ma clasps his shoulder. "It could save his life if you're better equipped at the fort."

Pa glances at you. "What do you think?"

Either option presents a risk. What do you decide?

If you want to try to rush him to Fort Boise, turn to page 147

If you want to treat him where you are, turn to page 66

You know you shouldn't ignore Pa. It'll be dark soon, and the oxen need to be unhitched. The wind is getting stronger, and you can already see clouds covering the horizon. But you don't want Matthew and Annie to think that you're afraid of adventure and the unknown. You bite your lip and continue to run after them.

"No, wait!" Ma points to the sky. "It's not safe!"

You're confident you'll be okay. You've been on the Trail for a few days, and you're getting the hang of everything. You'll be back to help with the evening chores soon.

"I'll be all right, Ma!" You wave.

Thunder rumbles overhead. Pa and Ma are both shouting, but you can barely hear them.

You turn just in time to see all six oxen barreling toward you. The storm has them shook. One of them knocks you to the ground. *Crunch!* You let out a cry.

Shocking pain sears down your leg. A one-thousand pound ox has trampled your foot as the oxen run toward the river.

You're hardly conscious as Ma and Pa carry you back to the wagon. You finally wake hours, maybe days, later, to find your entire leg in a sturdy splint.

"It's no use." Pa holds your hand. "Even though I set the leg as best I can, it'll take weeks, maybe even months, to heal. We'll have to head back to Independence."

All your dreams of adventure and opportunity on the Oregon Trail will have to wait until next year.

 **THE END**

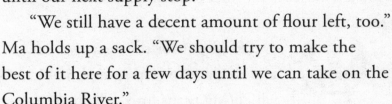

He can trap small animals, Pa," you say. "I'm sure there are deer around here too. We've got enough ammunition to hunt. We can find something to last us until our next supply stop."

"We still have a decent amount of flour left, too." Ma holds up a sack. "We should try to make the best of it here for a few days until we can take on the Columbia River."

Mr. Mason glowers. "Maybe we'll split up. *We* can afford the tollgate."

Pa shakes his head. "I wouldn't recommend splitting up, Mr. Mason. Not at this point. We're better off if we stay together. The Barlow Road can get very tricky, from what I've heard. It's not easy terrain."

"The doctor's right." Mrs. Mason looks at her husband. "Let's stay with the wagon train."

After a minute's deliberation, Mr. Mason

reluctantly agrees to remain with your wagon train. The Joneses choose to stay too. It would be foolish to go off on their own.

You're glad that everyone is sticking together. Taking the Barlow Toll Road would have been a mistake. Your family doesn't have much money left, and Pa will need new medical equipment for his new practice.

You hunt for the next two days and manage to trap several rabbits, which Ma turns into delicious stews. Pa makes a better splint for Mr. O'Neil's arm. Finally, your group continues on. You wander higher into the Blue Mountains. The bitter wind rushes through your bones. You bury your nose in a thick blanket, huddling between Annie and Matthew. Every part of you aches. Will you ever make it to Oregon City?

You travel around winding hills toward the Columbia River. Then, your wagon train stops atop a ridge. A spectacular vista spreads out before you:

the Columbia River Gorge. In the distant horizon to the west, you see the faint blue peak of Mount Hood rising above the other mountains.

It's one of the most incredible sights you've seen. You've wandered through prairies and deserts, forded rivers, and now climbed mountains. Your goal of reaching Oregon is so close—and it's even more beautiful than you could've imagined. Your long journey is almost at its end, but not quite.

Your wagon train descends the slope to The Dalles, which is long but thankfully not steep. The Columbia River has lowered in the past few days. You can tell from the banks of white sand by the river. As you reach the riverbank, you are struck by its enormity.

"Even if we build rafts, I'm not sure we can navigate that river." Pa stares across the rushing blue water.

"Back at Fort Boise, I heard there are guides you can pay to help you." Ma places her hands on Pa's back. "Maybe we could try to find someone?"

You're not sure if you can afford to hire a guide at this point. Plus, you know that taking the Barlow Road around Mount Hood will cost even more. No one in your wagon train knows how to navigate the powerful Columbia River. What should you do?

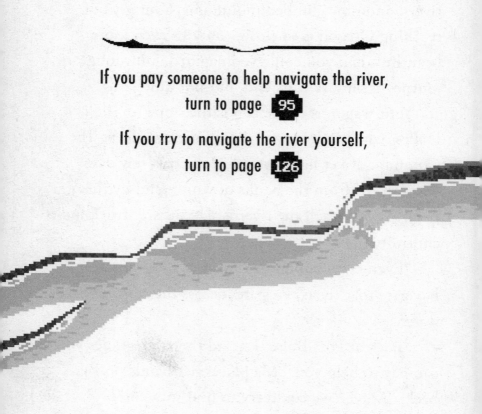

If you pay someone to help navigate the river, turn to page 95

If you try to navigate the river yourself, turn to page 126

You think about waiting, but when you and the Whittakers come across a pair of familiar wagons abandoned by the riverbank, you know they have already gone ahead without you. Everyone is hungry, tired, and grumpy from the weeks wasted going to and from the Barlow Road.

"We've already waited long enough." Mrs. Whittaker cradles William in her arms. "If we keep waiting, the weather might become worse than it already is."

You and your parents agree. You help Pa and Mr. Whittaker build a raft for both your families.

You, Annie, and Matthew will help Ma and Mrs. Whittaker steer the raft downriver, while Pa and Mr. Whittaker will drive the livestock alongside the riverbank.

As you place the last of your supplies onto the raft, you notice the clouds darkening overhead. Thunder rumbles nearby, and the rushing river darkens.

"Maybe this isn't a good idea." Annie shivers.

You shrug helplessly. She might be right, but it's too late now.

You leave your wagons behind and start off down the river as raindrops fall from the sky. You use long, heavy sticks to try to control your raft, but even with several people pushing and nudging at the riverbed, you're no match for the undercurrent. Your raft gains

speed, dipping into a bed of rapids, and slams into a sharp rock jutting out of the water.

Your raft spins out of control. Supplies fly everywhere. You hear shouts of surprise and alarm. You tumble off the raft as it flips over, tossing everyone into the rushing river. The current is too strong and pulls you under.

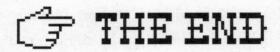 **THE END**

While the Barlow Road will be expensive and difficult, the alternative option sounds much too dangerous. Given the stretch of bad weather and the fact that the Columbia River is already hazardous enough, you don't want to risk losing more food or livestock.

Mr. O'Neil shakes his head sadly and motions to his broken arm. "I don't think I can travel right now, Doc. Think we're gonna have to stay here for a few days until I can start to feel a bit better. You understand."

Pa nods. "Of course. I'm sorry you can't come with us." He gives Mr. O'Neil some medicine to help with the pain. In the end, the Masons and the Whittakers stay with your wagon train, but the Joneses remain with the O'Neils. You're sad to part, but you're relieved that the O'Neils won't be alone in these mountains.

The next morning, you're on your way to the Barlow Road. The oxen still haven't fully recovered from the previous day's difficult travel. Your journey is slow through the rocky mountain terrain. You pass The Dalles and stop in the pleasant Tygh Valley. You rest for a full day before moving onward. You wish you could've stayed longer, but you know that your supplies are starting to run low. You have to reach the tollgate before the snows get too deep.

You emerge from the valley and wind your way through more mountains and snow-covered pine trees. Mount Hood finally comes into view, rising above the rest in a magnificent peak. As you climb higher, the snow gets deeper and thicker, and everyone grows more and more exhausted. You have to stop to let the oxen rest more often than you ever have.

To make matters worse, one of your wagon axles snaps. Mr. Whittaker helps you and Pa replace it, but that was your last spare axle. You'll have to spend even more money to buy a new one.

About a week later, you reach the tollgate station late in the afternoon. Your oxen are so tired from the steep climb that one of them collapses to the ground. It doesn't get up again, even when Pa and Mr. Whittaker rush to help it back up again, tempting it with water and food. It dies from pure exhaustion.

Now you're short one ox, and you still have to pay the exorbitant toll. But Pa returns from the station operator sooner than you would've thought.

"The price has gone up." Pa shakes his head. "It *was* five dollars per wagon and ten cents an ox. Now it's six dollars a wagon, because of the large number of wagons passing through this year. They know people don't have another safe route to Oregon City, and it's cruel."

"So how much would we have left, if we pay the toll?" You exchange worried glances with Ma.

"Not enough," he says. "We'll have to sell off some supplies—or two of our oxen."

"But we just lost one." Ma stomps the ground.

"I'm not sure what else we can do. With the way we've been rationing food, we need at least twenty pounds of food each." Pa cleans his spectacles with his kerchief. "What do you think?"

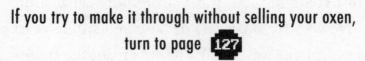

If you try to make it through without selling your oxen, turn to page **127**

If you sell your oxen, turn to page **101**

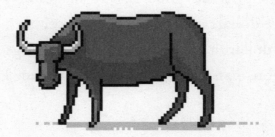

Most of your money was lost downstream. With what little you have left, you and your parents decide to trade what supplies you can spare for two new oxen.

"It's a loss, but we need to keep our current pace." Pa sighs heavily. "We can't afford to go slower than we are now."

As Pa goes to find two new oxen, you and Ma go into Big Springs' general store. The store owner, Mr. Dixon, warmly greets you. You tell him of your current situation.

"We see many pioneers come through here." Mr. Dixon adjusts his suspenders. "Some with much, some with very little. We're not a big fort or trading post, but we do what we can to supply travelers' needs."

Ma smiles. "It's a beautiful town. I can see why you settled here."

"Oh, it's not a large town, but a good one." He smiles. "That I can promise you. Folk are friendly."

"Pa's a doctor." You step up to the counter. "You wouldn't happen to need one of those, would you?"

Mr. Dixon's eyes widen. "Matter of fact, we do. Desperately. If y'all care to stay around, we'd be more than happy to have you."

Pa returns empty-handed, telling you that the other families are already planning on heading back to Independence. When you tell him of Big Springs' need of a doctor, his whole body loosens up. You may not be continuing on the Oregon Trail, but Big Springs is as good a place as any to settle down.

 **THE END**

While stopping is not the best idea, you know that Pa feels guilty about the wagon train splitting up once already.

You convince him to go to Salt Lake City. "We'll still get to California. But it'll be better if we stay together, don't you think?"

Pa and Ma agree with you.

"We've already let some people down." Pa's brow creases. "I'd hate to disappoint anyone else in our train. I'm sure it won't be too much out of our way. Can't hurt to stock up on more food and water while we're there too."

The remaining three wagons in your train start out early the next morning. It's roughly two hundred miles southeast to Salt Lake City. The journey is mostly uneventful. You're tired and dragging your feet by the time you arrive. But this sprawling city isn't like anywhere you've been before. It's surrounded by majestic snowcapped mountains that tower miles above the buildings and streets and trail off into the

distance. For a moment, you don't want to leave this beautiful place.

You've barely spent a few hours here wandering the streets and trading for supplies when Pa hurries up to you and Ma. His spectacles are crooked.

"I just learned that there's a bad cholera outbreak that's sweeping this city." Pa adjusts his spectacles.

Ma gasps. "That's horrible. What should we do?"

"The local doctor passed away from the cholera only a short time ago. They have no one else to help them. I'm wondering if I should stay to help, if I can."

"But aren't we supposed to keep moving on?" you ask. "We're still the wagon-train captains. What will the others say?"

Pa shakes his head. "I'm not sure. What do you think we should do, then? Should we stay and help, or keep passing through?"

You don't like how torn he looks. You know he wants to stay and help those in need. But you're also the leaders of your remaining wagon train. What should you do?

If you stay to help the community, turn to page **91**

If you want to keep passing through, turn to page **109**

You're not sure if hunting this herd of buffalo is a good idea. Then again, the O'Neils have more mouths to feed than anyone else in the wagon train. You feel guilty having so much more food available.

"Maybe we should let him," Ma whispers to Pa. "He might not have much food left."

Pa scratches his face. "We *have* been traveling a mighty long stretch without stopping at a fort or settlement. If there's a problem, I suppose we'll deal with it." He turns to Mr. O'Neil. "All right, I suppose you can hunt one buffalo. Just one. Make it quick."

Mr. O'Neil's face clears with relief. "Thank you, Doctor. I won't waste the meat, I promise."

He slowly slips down into the valley, armed

with his gun. But no sooner does he shoot and kill a buffalo than the five Arapaho men rush to meet him. Pa runs down to see what's going on. Soon, you can hardly hear anything above the shouting. But you know that Mr. O'Neil has made a terrible mistake—one that could cost you more than you thought.

The thunder of hoofbeats alerts you to the arrival of a platoon of soldiers. The captain jumps off his horse. After everyone has calmed down, you learn that things are worse than you could've imagined.

"You've broken a very serious treaty with the Arapaho Nation." The captain points at Pa and Mr. O'Neil. "They have a right to this herd of buffalo. Now that you've killed one of them, you'll have to pay a fine."

Pa rubs his chin wearily. "How much?"

Pa grows pale when he hears the amount.

"But that's all the money we have!" Mr. O'Neil protests.

"Then perhaps you'll be more careful hunting buffalo in the future," says the captain coldly.

Pa sighs. "You're right. Very well. We'll pitch in to help you, Mr. O'Neil."

But only you and the Whittakers agree to help the O'Neils pay the massive fine. The Masons and the Joneses refuse to pitch in, saying that they had nothing to do with it. Now, the O'Neils have no money left. And neither do you.

"We won't be able to buy more supplies." Pa kicks the dirt. "I don't even know if we would have anything valuable to trade."

Ma looks at you. "So what should we do? Should we keep going? Or should we try to go back to Big Springs? It's a small town. Maybe they need a doctor. Perhaps you could get some work there, at least for a short while."

"The O'Neils have nothing left either. They may try to return to Independence." Pa takes your hand. "What do you think? We could try making it through by hunting, maybe selling off animal hides and dried meat along the way."

Should you try to hunt as you travel the Oregon Trail and attempt to make money off animal skins, or go back to Big Springs?

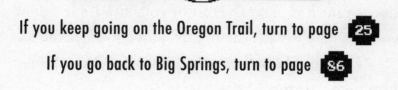

If you keep going on the Oregon Trail, turn to page **25**

If you go back to Big Springs, turn to page **86**

The young man doesn't look like he'd last more than two minutes in your wagon. In addition, you don't want him near the rest of your food. He might contaminate it with the highly contagious sickness.

"He should stay here, Pa," you say. "We can help him here at camp."

The day wears on as Pa carefully treats the young man. You rush to and from the nearest stream, helping Ma boil water and washing soiled blankets and linens. As night falls on your wagon corral, the young man is only getting sicker and weaker. To make matters even more complicated, the weather takes a sudden turn for the worse. Clouds coat the sky in a darkening gray shroud. The wind whips through your tents and wagon canvas, nearly blowing out your campfires. You shiver. It's gotten much colder all of a sudden.

Pa emerges from the young man's tent and shakes his head. He wipes off his spectacles. "I don't think

he'll last another hour. I've done everything I can to help, but it hasn't done much good."

You bite your cheek and glance up at the dark sky. "Weather doesn't look too good either, Pa."

"No, it doesn't." He frowns. "We might get a snowstorm."

That's the last thing you need. The other families have already been debating about whether or not they should leave; now you're certain they'll go on without you. Sure enough, thick, fat snowflakes start falling, covering the ground in seconds. The wind whistles through the grass.

Mrs. Whittaker rushes over to your family. You have a feeling that something is terribly wrong.

"It's my husband." Her cheeks are pink. "He's sick. Vomiting and feverish. And Annie says her stomach is hurting her now too. Dr. Howard, you have to help us. Is it cholera?"

Pa hurries over to their tents. You're terrified that

Mrs. Whittaker is right. Pa returns some time later, his head hung low. "The Whittaker family and now two members of the O'Neil family have contracted cholera. I'll need your help—and your ma's—now more than ever."

Only an hour later, you find Pa collapsed just outside his tent. You shout for Ma. She's been helping the Whittaker family, but she now runs back at your call. The two of you cover Pa in blankets. He's shivering and very pale.

"What should we do, Ma?" You know he's contracted cholera.

"I should go get help at Fort Boise." Ma pulls on her bonnet. "I don't think we'll make it with everyone getting sick like this."

The snow is already piling up outside, showing no signs of letting up. You're worried Ma might not even make it to the fort. What do you do?

If you try to get help at Fort Boise, turn to page 23

If you wait out the snowstorm, turn to page 88

Cholera sounds like a risk you don't want to take. It's a disease that isn't easily cured. Most people die within a day, even if they were perfectly healthy several hours earlier.

"We should try for the Santa Fe Trail," you suggest. "We've barely started out on our trek, Pa. If we get sick . . ."

Pa doesn't seem entirely convinced. "But the practice is waiting for me in Oregon City—"

"I'm sure you can start your own practice in Santa Fe," Ma says. "The practice in Oregon City will understand."

Finally, Pa agrees with you and Ma. "All right. We'll try it out in Santa Fe. Hopefully they need as many doctors as Oregon City."

After a wagon-train discussion, only you and the Whittakers decide to head for Santa Fe. The other three families in your wagon train argue that taking the Santa Fe Trail does not guarantee safety.

"Safety in numbers," says Mr. Jones. "Splitting up is not a good idea, Doctor."

Pa shakes his head. "I have to do what's best for my family. I know you'd do the same."

You watch the other wagons disappear over the horizon and an uneasiness settles in your stomach. You hope your family made the right decision. Bandits are common on the trails, and fewer people means it will be harder to keep watch at night.

You and the Whittakers start off on the Santa Fe Trail, heading south. One night, you wake to the sound of shouting. Bandits surround your tiny makeshift corral. You're forced to give up all your money and many valuable supplies—and your dreams of ever getting to Oregon City.

☞ **THE END**

Thank you," you tell the trader, "but I think I'll check with my ma first."

The man glares at you and stomps out of the general store.

Ma waves you over. "Tajé Mi and Ke Wák'o were just telling me that that man's a notorious swindler. The authorities have been trying to catch him for months. They just went to warn the soldiers outside to have him arrested."

You're relieved you didn't buy anything from *him!*

"I told him I was going to ask you first," you say.

Ma smiles. "I'm proud of you for that. It was a wise thing to do."

You and Ma stock up on supplies: you get four hundred more pounds of food, including flour, more bacon, and even sugar.

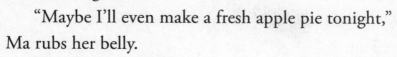

"Maybe I'll even make a fresh apple pie tonight," Ma rubs her belly.

Your mouth waters.

When you and Ma reunite with Pa outside in the town square, you find him treating one of the soldiers in a small platoon.

"Hard to keep a wagon train together." The soldier waves his arms. "Disease . . . starvation . . . arguments, even . . . I've seen wagon trains come and go. Most don't make it without losing at least a few folk."

Pa frowns. "Well, we haven't lost anyone so far. I know we've hardly begun, but I think we can make it if we stay together." He finishes wrapping the bandage around the soldier's leg.

"Stay together, Doctor," says the soldier. "Most important thing you can do."

Later on, Pa tells you that the soldiers have been very helpful in pointing out the best direction. "They said the path ahead up to Fort Caspar and Fort Hall is crossing difficult terrain. But they have treaties with the Pawnee and Arapaho Nations in this region. We should take care to ration food before the next settlement."

After two days of rest, your wagon train starts

moving on the Trail again. You're sad to leave the pleasant little town of Big Springs, but then you think of Oregon City and that fuels your will to travel on.

You trek for miles and miles. You make sure to ration your food from fair to meager portions. You miss having more than one piece of bacon, but you have to conserve as much food as possible.

One afternoon, you come across a herd of buffalo grazing in a valley. One family calls out to stop. It's a family of farmers, the O'Neils. They have five little children, all younger than you. Like you and Pa, Mr. O'Neil hunts for jackrabbits and antelope on the plains when you stop to rest. But he has more mouths to feed than Pa, and wild game is scarce.

"'Scuse me, Dr. Howard." Mr. O'Neil approaches your wagon "Those are mighty fine buffalo. Shame to let all that meat go to waste when it's just sitting there."

Pa pushes his spectacles up his nose. "They seem to be herded already. Notice how they're encased in a valley."

"Exactly!" Mr. O'Neil licks his lips. "My family and I could use the meat, not to mention all those buffalo chips for building a fire."

You look around over the ridge. You remember hearing something about the local Arapaho Nation in this area having treaties with the soldiers. You've also heard from passing traders in Independence and Big Springs that different Plains Nations have rights to these herds of buffalo.

"Maybe we should wait and see," you suggest.

Mr. O'Neil stomps his foot. "Wait for what, exactly?"

"Look!" You point to the top of the ridge, where five Arapaho men sit on horseback. "I think they have a right to this herd of buffalo."

Pa squints into the sunlight. "Hmm. I think you might be correct."

"You don't know that." Mr. O'Neil's face is red. "Maybe they're waitin' to hunt those buffalo like the rest of us. There's plenty of 'em to go around. Plenty. We don't need much meat, anyway."

"I'm not sure we should interfere." Pa wipes his brow.

"Just one buffalo," Mr. O'Neil insists. "That's it, Doctor. Can't hurt to kill just *one* buffalo, can it?"

You're not sure. What should your family do?

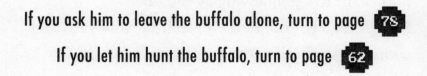

If you ask him to leave the buffalo alone, turn to page **78**

If you let him hunt the buffalo, turn to page **62**

You're so close to Oregon City. It's not much farther to continue down the Willamette River to your final destination. You've got to keep moving. Everyone can rest when you get to Oregon City. You don't want to lose momentum now.

The O'Neils disagree at first. They want to stop in Fort Vancouver to get supplies. The Joneses support their decision, but the Whittakers and the Masons both want to keep moving as you do.

Ultimately, you decide to split up your rafts and continue on ahead without the two families. Your Klickitat guide named Ow-hi tells you that he wants to end his journey with you in Fort Vancouver rather than go all the way down the Willamette River to Oregon City. You say farewell to him when you get to the fort. Now you must navigate the rest of the way on your own.

At first, this leg of the journey goes smoothly. Pa, Mr. Whittaker, and Mr.

Mason continue to herd the livestock along the riverbank while you and the others drive the raft down the river.

The weather takes a turn for the worse. The wind picks up, and rain pours down in sheets. Before you know it, the raft is pulled under by the river current. You and the others are left floundering for shore. It's a miracle that no one drowns, but all your supplies and food are floating downstream. You may be alive, but your dreams of Oregon City drown in this river.

☞ THE END

Hunting this herd of buffalo doesn't sound like a good idea, especially with the Arapaho men on the other side of the valley.

"Remember what the soldiers said, Pa," you say. "They have treaties with the Nations in this area. If we hunt buffalo, there could be trouble. We don't want that, do we?"

Pa shakes his head. "No, we certainly don't." He wipes dust off his spectacles and turns to Mr. O'Neil. "If you're running low on supplies, we'll be happy to share. But we need to leave these buffalo alone. We'll stop a few miles up ahead. There might be more buffalo or some antelopes, even."

"But . . ." Mr. O'Neil stops himself. "All right. We'll keep going." He hauls his gun over his shoulder and returns to his wagon.

As you start moving again, George Washington barks. You look over to see one of the Arapaho men waving. You smile, knowing you did the right thing.

Only a few miles later, you find a small herd of deer grazing. Pa and several of the other men retrieve the meat from three bucks, which will last several days among the six wagons. You, Annie, and Matthew help pick up dried patches of buffalo dung, or "buffalo chips," which you'll use as kindling for campfires.

"Chips or not, it's still manure," Matthew snickers.

Annie rolls her eyes, and you laugh.

You eventually make it to Fort Bridger, where you rest for a day, restock on supplies, and continue on. You cross canyons and rivers. Your wagon gets a broken axle. Mr. Whittaker helps you and Pa replace it, but now you have only one extra left.

Weeks later, you reach Fort Hall. It's bustling with excitement. There are soldiers, traders, Cheyenne families, and other wagon trains stopping there before moving on to either Oregon, Salt Lake City, or California. You hear people murmuring about the Gold Rush.

You smile as a young girl eagerly scratches your Newfoundlands' shaggy heads. She's wearing clothing of the Cheyenne Nation.

"They're friendly." You smile.

She sneaks them a piece of buffalo jerky just before your ma calls you away. You wave goodbye. You wish you could stay longer, but you're here for only a few days. Pa buys a new replacement axle, and Ma stocks up on more food. She even cooks soft, doughy biscuits and a fresh apple pie. Your favorite!

On the second day, you're milking Trixie while Ma and Pa are loading food onto the wagon.

Mr. Whittaker approaches. "Listen, Doctor, some of the other families and I have been talking. We've been thinking that we might try to head south to California instead of north to Oregon. Trail might be a bit easier, and there might be more opportunity, given the Gold Rush."

Pa's eyes widen. "You really think it's a wise idea to change trails now? Gold is hardly a guaranteed prospect, Mr. Whittaker."

"Well, we've depleted more funds than we would've liked. You know we had to chuck some of my bigger tools along the way. I'm not sure I have enough money to buy new ones when we get to Oregon City. If we happen to strike gold out in California—"

"That's a big 'if.'" Ma steps beside Pa.

Mr. Whittaker nods. "I know. But . . . we're seriously considering it. Would you folks be willing to split up and go with us and the O'Neils to California?"

You remember hearing about people heading

to California in droves, but not everyone winds up striking gold. In fact, you've been hearing murmurs around the fort that the Gold Rush may be over.

Should you agree to split up and try for California, or try to convince everyone to keep going on the Oregon Trail?

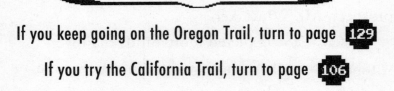

If you keep going on the Oregon Trail, turn to page **129**

If you try the California Trail, turn to page **106**

Although you're concerned about the fur traders returning, you know the oxen won't make it more than a few miles.

"We'll have a better chance if we keep watch tonight," you offer. "That's what being in a wagon train is all about, right, Pa? Making sure we look after one another?"

Pa and Ma share a smile.

"You're absolutely right." Pa hugs you to his side. "Especially as leaders of the train, we need to ensure everyone's well-being. We have a better chance of that by staying in a strong corral."

That night, Pa and the other men keep watch around the circle of wagons. In the middle of the night, you hear something just outside your tent. George Washington and King George whimper, then growl. You scramble outside to see one of the fur traders sneaking toward your wagon!

You shout for

your pa. He and Mr. Whittaker rush over. They scare off the "fur traders."

"Good work!" They pat you on the back.

You scratch your dogs' heads. "The Georges helped!"

King George rewards you with an especially slobbery kiss.

The next morning, there's still excitement over last night's hubbub, but you've all overslept and get a late start to the day. You hurry to scribble everything down in your family's journal as Ma and Pa cook a hasty breakfast. The camp is chaotic.

You stuff your face with johnnycakes—a flat cornmeal cake cooked on the griddle—and bacon as quickly as you can. Now you're very thirsty. The food tastes a bit funny, but you're so hungry, you don't complain. Maybe it wasn't cooked enough, but you know everyone is in a hurry to make up for lost time and get to Big Springs.

A few hours into traveling, both Pa and Ma

complain of stomach cramps. Soon, your wagon has to stop. Pa and Ma are shaking and throwing up. They both have a fever and they're too sick to go on. With Pa being the only doctor, no one else knows how to help them.

"Maybe there's a doctor in Big Springs." Mrs. Whittaker pulls at her bonnet. "We could go get help."

You're not sure what to do. Pa has taught you some medical information. Should you try to find another doctor or help them yourself?

If you try to get help at Big Springs, turn to page **117**

If you try to help them yourself, turn to page **118**

I don't think we'll make it trying to trap animals for trade, Pa," you admit. Pa is a doctor. He's never been an especially good hunter, and none of you knows the first thing about trading for a living along the Oregon Trail. Back home you lived in a busy town—you haven't had much practice killing and skinning animals.

Pa nods. "I don't think we would. We should try to head back to Big Springs. Maybe I can get work as a doctor there. I'm sure lots of passing pioneers will need our help."

But Mr. Mason and the Joneses are upset by this prospect.

"You're just going to turn back?" Mr. Mason says. "You were supposed to be our wagon-train captain, Doctor!"

Pa shrugs helplessly. "I'm sorry. There's nothing else we can do."

Mr. Mason storms off. "I'm sorry we ever joined this wagon train. A lot of good it's done us."

Your family and the Whittakers are the only ones to head back to Big Springs. The Masons and the Joneses decide to hunt animals and sell their fur along the Trail. You finally make it back to Big Springs, where Pa sets up a small practice caring for the tiny community, along with any passing wagon trains. It's not the life you'd hoped for, but it'll do until you can try for Oregon City next year.

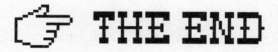 **THE END**

You shake your head. "No, Ma, don't go. It's snowing too much. We should try to wait it out."

Pa opens his eyes and nods weakly. "Don't go out in this. You could get stuck in the snow." He trembles and pulls his blanket tighter around himself.

"Hush!" Ma wraps her scarf around him. "Don't talk. You need to rest."

But you and she both know there's little either of you can do.

"Here, Pa—drink some water." You hold a steaming-hot cup to his lips.

Before he takes one sip, he doubles over. Ma moves to help him. Your heart fills with worry. Maybe trying to brave the storm would have been the wiser option—that is, if your own brain weren't so fuzzy. Now you're shaking. Within hours, you die of cholera.

 **THE END**

We've done all the work we can here, Pa," you say. "Salt Lake City is nice, but we should keep going to California."

Ma smiles. "I'll echo that. It feels like we've been here for years, not days. Let's move on."

You meet up with the other two families, who are relieved to finally be pushing forth on the California Trail after delaying for so long.

"We're sure glad you decided to come along, Doc," Mr. O'Neil admits. "Thought you were going to settle here for good."

Pa shakes his head. "Just performing my Hippocratic oath, Mr. O'Neil. But we're ready to be your wagon captains once again."

You're not even twenty miles out when disaster strikes. Mrs. Whittaker comes across a snake in the brush. It bites her ankle. Pa tries to save her, but he's too late. She dies several days later. Her children are devastated. Mr. Whittaker announces he's going back to Salt Lake City.

"Don't think we'll make it out to California now." Tears fill his eyes.

You're sad to say goodbye to Annie and Matthew. You and the O'Neils press on. An axle on your wagon breaks, and you're not sure how to fix it. Mr. Whittaker was the carpenter, but now he's gone. Mr. O'Neil and Pa eventually replace it, but the wagon never moves as smoothly as it did before.

You eventually run short on water. Two of your oxen die of dehydration. To make matters worse, you're so exhausted and thirsty that you forget to tie up Trixie one night. She wanders off into the desert. You never find her again.

You hope you'll make it to California eventually, but the second half of your journey has been riddled with heartache and disaster. You never should have split up your wagon train and left the Oregon Trail.

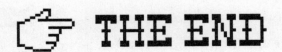 **THE END**

These people need our help, Pa," you say. "It wouldn't be right to just leave when everyone's so sick and in need of a doctor."

Pa rolls up his sleeves and wipes his brow. "You're absolutely right. It's our duty to do what's best for these poor people."

Ma smiles and squeezes your shoulder. "We'll make it to California eventually. I'm proud of you for understanding what's really important."

The three of you find a nearby inn to stay and board your team of oxen—and Trixie, of course— while you set up a makeshift practice to help the suffering community. You and Ma act as Pa's

assistants, running to and fro to help him change linens and towels. You retrieve water from the nearby spring and boil it to make sure it's clean. The patients' area is as comfortable and sterile as possible.

It's not pleasant work, and many people still die of cholera. But you know that you're making a difference and manage to help save several lives. You make sure to tell people to always boil their water, to avoid alkaline water at all costs, and to eat only fully cooked food.

The Whittakers and the O'Neils aren't pleased about lingering in Salt Lake City for so long. On the fourth day in the city, both families come and find you.

"Doc, we know you're trying to do good here," Mr. O'Neil says. "But we gotta keep moving on. We're honestly afraid of getting cholera ourselves."

"We have to think about our own families."

Mrs. Whittaker clutches little William tightly. "This place is riddled with sickness. We can't stay here. If you intend on living here, we'll move on without you."

Pa wipes his brow and looks to you and Ma. "We didn't plan on staying here for good, Mrs. Whittaker. But . . . let me talk it over with my family, and I'll let you all know."

"By tonight!" Mr. Whittaker slams his fist on the counter. "We're leaving first thing tomorrow morning, with or without you, Dr. Howard."

Later that day, you receive a sudden influx of patients that leaves you and your parents overwhelmed with work. You barely have time to breathe, much less think about packing up and going back on the Trail. Despite all the hard work, you start to get to know the families in the community, who are grateful to have a physician in the area. You feel good knowing you're helping, and you start to make new friends.

That night, you and your parents sit around a table at the inn's tavern, worn out and unsure of what to do. You like Salt Lake City. The people are friendly, and it's a pleasant climate.

Should you stay here for a while longer or keep going with the other two families along the California Trail?

If you stay in Salt Lake City, turn to page **29**

If you keep moving along the California Trail, turn to page **89**

Most of you are running low on funds, but finding a guide to help navigate the river is worth the price. You pool some money together and locate a guide nearby.

Soon enough, you meet a Klickitat man named Ow-hi who agrees to navigate your rafts through the rocky river gorge. You help Ma, Pa, and the others build two large rafts for the wagon train—you'll have to leave your wagons behind. Ow-hi will be on the raft with you, the Whittakers, and the Masons, while the O'Neils and the Joneses will follow on the other raft.

But not even Ow-hi can get you past a deadly stretch of rapids called the Cascades, nearly thirty miles ahead. About four miles long, the rapids are far too steep for any raft or canoe. Ow-hi tells everyone that the Cascades must be portaged, meaning the supplies must be carried overland for a short period.

"But that's impossible!" Mr. Mason shakes his fist. "We have far too much to carry!" He waves to his two wagons.

"There will be others to help," Ow-hi promises. "It will not be an easy path, but it is the only way around the rapids."

Mr. Mason wrinkles his nose.

Pa clasps a strong hand onto your shoulder. "I'm glad you'll have someone to help you. I feel better knowing the journey will be safer for everyone."

"What do you mean?" Your eyebrows raise.

"Ow-hi tells us that it's safer to drive the stock on the bank of the river alongside you and meet you at the portage. Which is why I'm counting on you to listen to Ow-hi and help your ma raft our wagon's cargo safely down the river. Can you do that?"

You nod and swallow. This will be even more difficult than you thought.

Finally, all five families are on the two rafts, and

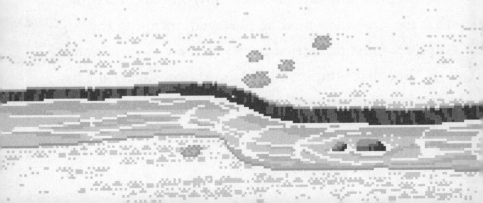

Mr. O'Neil has the stock herded off on the riverbank. You start out on the Columbia River. The rafts are precarious. You're afraid that they will tip over in a watery whirlpool. Everything you have will be lost.

You and Ma follow Ow-hi's instructions to carefully navigate through the stony river, around fallen logs and rougher undercurrents that can tip your raft.

Herded alongside you on the riverbank are the oxen, your cow, Trixie, and the rest of the wagon-train stock. Even your two beloved dogs remain on land, helping Pa and the other men keep the animals close together. You wish you had at least one of your dogs with you on the raft to make you feel a bit better.

Just when you thought you couldn't get any more

anxious, thunder booms overhead and rain pours.
You can hardly see two feet in front of you. At least
Ow-hi knows the river. He helps your raft avoid small
rapids and rocky patches.

Even so, your raft catches on the side of a sharp
rock and dips down. You let out a shout as you
stumble toward the water. Holding on to the raft, you
catch your breath but your foot slips into the water.
The current catches your shoe and carries it away.

"Are you all right?" Ma grabs your shoulder.

You nod, your fingers are numb from gripping
the raft so tightly. You see socks, a tablecloth, and
Ma's favorite milk jug bobbing past you down the
river. When you hear a sorrowful cry from Mrs.
O'Neil, you know that you're not the only raft to
have lost important supplies.

You've never been so happy to step on land when
you reach the portage. There are men there already

helping other pioneers carry their cargo and haul canoes and rafts across land. After they help you cross a slippery, narrow stretch of terrain, you're able to get back on a more manageable section of the river, with the Cascades behind you. You lose sight of Pa and the others on land from time to time, but you're relieved when you hear King George and George Washington's cheerful barks echoing nearby.

Finally, you emerge from the Columbia River Gorge, and you and the other raft dock by the riverbank to take a short break on land. Pa and the others catch up to you. Everyone shares a quick meal of coffee and johnnycakes. You have to borrow some cornmeal from the Whittakers. Yours spilled into the river.

"I know everyone lost something in the river." Ma stokes the fire. "Fort Vancouver is a little ways downriver. What if we stop there to restock before reaching Oregon City?"

At this point, everyone is too exhausted and too uncertain to know which would be a better decision. While you want nothing more than to reach Oregon City, you'd really like a new pair of shoes, and a decent meal to keep up your strength for the final leg of the journey. What should you do?

If you keep going directly to Oregon City, turn to page 76

If you stop at Fort Vancouver, turn to page 160

We can still try to make it with just three oxen, Pa," you say. "But we can't make it without food."

"You're absolutely right." Ma folds an empty sack of flour. "I don't like the idea of having fewer oxen, but we do need to make sure that we have an ample supply of food."

Pa nods. "You're right. But I wouldn't be surprised if their supplies are more expensive here than back at Fort Boise. We're in the middle of the mountains."

"Let's hope not too expensive." Ma shakes out a towel.

Unfortunately, Pa is right. One pound of flour is three times the price of what it was in Fort Boise. Not only do you have to sell off two oxen, but you also have to sell your cow, Trixie. You're

upset to give up your wandering dairy cow— and the luxury of fresh milk every morning—but you need food staples more than anything else. Pa, already irritated at the increased toll fee, is furious at the station's prices and argues with the store owner for hours. But there's nothing you can do.

When you're finally ready to leave, Annie and Matthew come up to you.

"We had to sell our horse." Annie frowns. "And even then, it wasn't enough."

"What do you mean?" You tilt your head.

Matthew kicks at a pebble. "We don't have enough money to buy more food. Pa says we have to stay here and pay back what we owe for the food we did buy. He has to work here at the station for a couple months to settle our debt."

You're shocked. But you know that you've barely been able to afford the tollgate. "So . . . you're not coming with us."

They both shake their heads.

You and the Masons continue on past the tollgate,

but attempting to descend down the incredibly steep Laurel Hill costs you another ox. Short on money and oxen, you decide to turn around to go back to the Barlow Gate. Pa can try to be a physician to the passing pioneers until you can save up money for new oxen. You can try again for Oregon City next year.

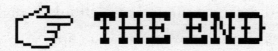 **THE END**

You're not sure if the other two wagons have gone on without you, but with the clap of thunder overhead and the river rushing by, you think it might be better to wait until the weather clears up.

You and the Whittakers set up camp near the riverbank, eager to eat and rest. You, Matthew, and Annie skip rocks in the river, but Pa warns you not to get too close. The river is rising quickly. You have to move your wagons to higher ground later that day as the weather worsens. You've never been so cold or miserable in your life as you huddle in your tent that night.

In the morning, you wake up to a horrified shout. You hurry outside, bleary-eyed. The river is rushing past you only feet away—and both your wagon and the Whittakers' have disappeared.

"Carried off by the river," Pa says grimly. "We were in too much of a hurry to set up camp. We were too close to the riverside."

At this point, it'll be impossible to make it to Oregon City without wagons and supplies.

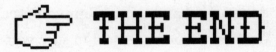 **THE END**

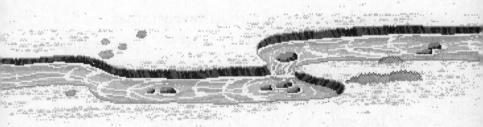

It's your job to lead the wagon train to Oregon City. If you split up now, you'll be abandoning those families who don't want to go to California, and Pa will be giving up the practice waiting for him in Oregon City.

On the other hand, you've heard good things about California. The climate is pleasant all year round; the opportunities are plentiful . . . Maybe it's a good idea, after all.

"Why don't we try it, Pa? Maybe that way we can avoid the Blue Mountains and the Columbia River."

Ma nods. "You have a point. And I'm sure you can open up your own practice wherever we settle down. I like the thought of warmer weather."

Pa adjusts his spectacles. "Well . . . I'm not sure I like the idea of changing our course so suddenly, but if it's what you want . . . let's do it."

In the end, the Whittakers and the O'Neils decide to go with you to California. The Masons and the Joneses are adamant about continuing on the Oregon Trail.

"You were our wagon captain." Mr. Mason puts his hands on his hips. "You promised to lead us to Oregon City. What will we do now if something happens to one of us?"

Pa shakes his head guiltily. "I'm sorry, Mr. Mason. I've done my best."

As you're about to leave, another issue arises. Not everyone wants to head straight out on the California Trail. The O'Neils want to stop in Salt Lake City to make sure they have enough supplies for the desert road ahead.

"But Salt Lake City is backtracking," Ma argues. "We'd be much better off just continuing on the California Trail from here. I'm sure we can find another fort along the way."

Mrs. O'Neil shakes her head. "Salt Lake City is the last major stopping point. We have to make sure we're fully prepared. So far we've been fortunate, but who knows what we'll encounter going south?"

She has a point. Maybe you should stop at Salt Lake City, even though it is out of your way. You'll have to go much farther south and backtrack slightly east. If you decide to start out on the California Trail straight from here, you'll have to split up what's left of your wagon train again. You may be striking out on the Trail alone, and that's never a good thing.

Should you stop in Salt Lake City first, or split up the wagon train to start out on the California Trail?

If you stop in Salt Lake City, turn to page 59

If you start out on the California Trail, turn to page 27

We should keep moving." Your palms sweat. Pa has told you and Ma how incredibly contagious cholera is. The last thing your family needs is to contract the deadly disease.

Pa chews on his lip. "Well . . . I suppose it's for the best. I'm sure there are other doctors nearby who can help."

Ma nods. "You're right. We should keep moving if we want to make it to California before the summer sun heats up the desert and dries up our water sources."

Before you leave, Ma gives you a little bit of spending money to use at the fort. You're so hungry, and a snack sounds perfect before you head back on the Trail. You see a  haggard-looking woman rotating a chicken over a fire pit. You wonder if you should just move on, but you haven't had chicken in so long. You buy half a chicken and eagerly dig in. It tastes a little funny, but you keep eating.

Several miles out on the California Trail, you have stomach cramps. Before you know it, you're really sick. You shouldn't have eaten that chicken.

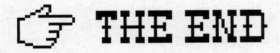 **THE END**

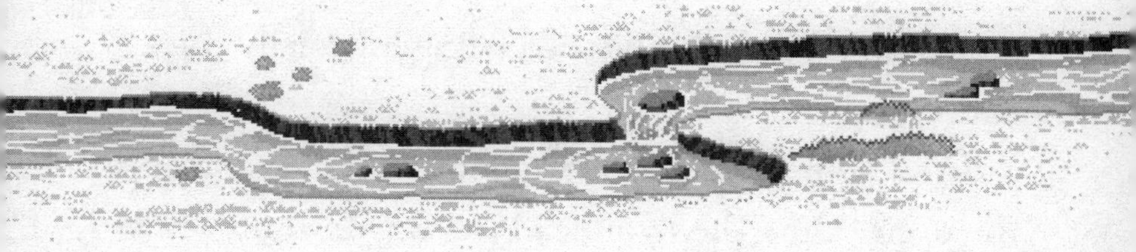

That river looks pretty dangerous, Pa. We should wait a bit until it gets lower, don't you think?"

Pa nods. "It would be a mistake to cross it right now." He turns back to Mr. Whittaker and Mr. Mason. "If you need any supplies or food, Mr. Mason, I'm sure we can all pitch in to help out. But we must wait at least a day before crossing the river, until it calms down some."

Mr. Whittaker's face softens. "I agree. I can help with any repairs needed."

Mr. Mason throws up his hands.

You return to camp and salvage what you can of the flour. You wait a day and see the river getting lower, but it's still too high to cross. After the third day, the river has finally quieted to a level of about three feet. You could try to ford it with the wagons as they are, but you remember reading what the trail

guide said about the riverbed being especially thick
and muddy.

You help Pa caulk the wagon with tar and keep
the oxen calm. Then you lead the wagon train across
the river, down one steep riverbank and back up the
other. Pa and Mr. Whittaker have already crossed the
river and tie ropes to strong trees to tow the wagons
up the limestone incline. It's a long, slow process.
Two of the wagons still lose some supplies to the
river, but everyone makes it to the other side safely.

"We did it!" You jump up and down as the
Georges race up the riverbank, barking loudly.

Annie and Matthew follow close by.

"Are we almost there?" Matthew asks hopefully.

Annie laughs. "We just started, silly."

Matthew frowns.

It's only about six miles to Hogback Ridge, but
the next day you notice the pleasantly flat prairie
growing hillier. Soon, you find yourselves going up
and down rolling hills dotted with thick trees and
golden-white stone.

"Limestone." Pa points to the trail. "Looks like this area is covered with it."

The oxen begin to struggle going up the rocky slopes. One is particularly difficult. Just beyond this incline, an enormous, never-ending hill rises above all the others.

"Hogback Ridge." Pa looks into the distance. "It's also called Devil's Backbone."

Matthew gallops up next to you. It's his turn to ride their horse. "Race you to the top?"

You grin. "After you!"

Your wagon train pauses for a brief midday respite. As George Washington and King George play with little William Whittaker, you help Ma get some water from a nearby stream and boil it for coffee.

Mr. Mason, his wife, and one other wagon-train family come up to your wagon.

"Dr. Howard, we'd like a word." Mr. Mason tips his hat.

You resist rolling your eyes. Mr. Mason has something to say every single time you stop.

Pa turns from milking Trixie. "Yes?"

"We've been checking the map, and we're thinking that we should avoid going over Devil's Backbone altogether. If we keep to lower ground, avoid the hill country, we can still get to Big Springs without having to cross that monstrous ridge. Look." He places the map on the ground.

You frown, studying the map. "I'm not sure that's such a good idea, Mr. Mason. We've already climbed high enough that once we cross over  Hogback Ridge, we'll be able to stay on top of the hills and avoid going up and down over and over."

"You might be right." Pa then turns to the Masons. "Big Springs is still in hill country. You'll wear the oxen out if you go back to low ground."

Mr. Mason and the others aren't convinced.

"We'll wear the oxen out going over Devil's Backbone," Mrs. Mason interjects.

She has a point. The oxen still haven't fully

recovered from their slog through the Wakarusa
River. Should you convince the others that you
should go over Devil's Backbone, or take their
suggested route downhill?

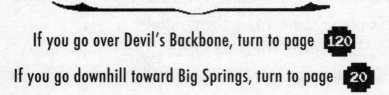

If you go over Devil's Backbone, turn to page **120**

If you go downhill toward Big Springs, turn to page **20**

Your parents' fevers are running hotter, and it's only a matter of hours before it's too late. Even though you dread leaving your family, you can't bear to wait and do nothing.

You tell the Whittakers that you're going to try to find a doctor in Big Springs. It's a popular town for travelers on the Oregon Trail—they must have someone who can help.

"We can't let you go by yourself." Mrs. Whittaker's face glows by the campfire.

"I'll be fine." You ignore the sudden queasy rolling in your stomach. "Can I borrow your horse? I promise I'll return it."

Annie brings the horse around. "Be careful. You don't look so good yourself."

You thank her but brush off her warning. You gallop off into the hills. But fever consumes you. You never make it to Big Springs.

"I can try to help them," you say bravely. "I think they have dysentery." The food this morning wasn't cooked enough. In such a hurry to leave, Pa and Ma weren't paying attention to breakfast. You swallow, feeling suddenly queasy. You ate the same food. You thought it tasted funny. You can't get sick too!

Mrs. Whittaker steps back. "Dysentery? Can that be cured?"

"Pa's taught me some things." You hurry to grab Pa's doctor bag out of the back of the wagon. "If we wait too long, it might be too late."

"Let us know if we can do anything to help." Mrs. Whittaker places a hand on your shoulder. You know the rest of the wagon train wants to keep moving, especially away from any disease and illness.

Even though you try to give Pa and Ma medicine from his medical bag, nothing helps. They can't keep it down. Their fevers get higher.

Your own stomach gurgles after a few hours. You take medicine, but you know it's already too late.

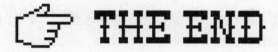 **THE END**

If we keep going and climb Devil's Backbone now, we'll stay on top of the hills. That way we won't be going up and down and up and down." You convince the Masons that going down into the valley would tire out the oxen more quickly.

"You may be right." Mrs. Mason mounts her wagon. "Let's try it. The sooner we get to Big Springs, the better."

Pa and Ma smile at you. You can't help but feel a little proud of yourself.

The journey up Devil's Backbone is a long, slow, and steady climb. Step by step, you rise higher. Your feet ache, and your head begins to pound. But the thought of reaching the next town pushes you forward. You can see more rolling hills stretch across the horizon and, in the very faint distance, smoke nestled in the countryside.

The Georges trot alongside the wagon, their noses to the ground, sniffing for scents of antelope and prairie dogs. King George lies on the grass and rolls around, his long tongue hanging to one side.

You laugh. At least you're not the only one who's tired.

Finally, you see the peak of Devil's Backbone in sight. Your legs burn, but you know you still have a long way to go after this. Annie and Matthew hurry up to you.

"C'mon." Annie runs beside you. "Race both of you to the top!"

You glance at Ma, who nods and smiles.

"You don't stand a chance!" You take off up the hill.

In the end, it's the Georges who sprint ahead and claim Kings of the Hill, barking and wagging their tails. You, Annie, and Matthew fall to the ground, out of breath.

"I never want to see another hill again." Annie catches her breath.

"You're telling me," Matthew pants.

"I just did, silly."

Your wagon train stops to rest for the night atop Devil's Backbone. You, Annie, and Matthew scratch your names into a nearby limestone rock.

"There." You step back to view your work. "Now other travelers will know we've been here."

"We've conquered Devil's Backbone!" Matthew jumps.

"We still have to go back down," Annie reminds him.

He sticks out his tongue.

The next day, Pa pulls you aside. "The terrain up ahead will be tricky. We have to make sure we keep the oxen as calm as possible. I need you to stay by my side at all times. Do you understand?"

You nod, although you're sad you can't walk

alongside Annie and Matthew today. They'd wanted to play games on the Trail. Games will have to wait.

For the next several hours, you help Pa carefully lead the oxen over the rolling hills toward Big Springs. The terrain, while still somewhat difficult, is much easier than it would have been had you descended into the valley yesterday. The tired oxen never would have made it back up these hills. In addition, there are many clear, fresh springs nearby. The oxen drink greedily when they can.

"I think this is what Big Springs gets its name from." Pa rinses his hands in the water. "I've heard this area is an exceptional watering location due to its plentiful springs."

You want to drink, but you should boil it first, just to be safe.

Finally, you come along a more gradual slope that leads up to a tiny town square, with a general store, a blacksmith, a church, and a wagon-repair shop.

"It should be called Small Springs," you whisper to Pa.

He smiles.

Small or not, Big Springs is a pleasant town with about forty residents in total. There are some traders and soldiers passing through. It's a good place to check your location on the map and stock up on supplies.

Pa and Mr. Whittaker head over to the small platoon of soldiers to ask about the journey ahead. You want to go with him, but Ma needs your help getting goods at the general store.

Ma talks to the man behind the counter and meets two Native American women of the Kansa Nation. You are looking at the shelved goods when you come across a tall man with a big fur-covered hat.

"Hey, kid." He's holding a stack of blankets. "It'll get cold up in them mountains. You should get some of these. Nice and warm. Reckon you don't want to freeze to death."

Ma gave you a little spending money, but you should ask her first before buying anything. You also want to prove you're old enough to be responsible. What should you do?

If you buy blankets, turn to page **18**

If you ask Ma first, turn to page **71**

You may not be familiar with the Columbia River, but your family doesn't have much money left. You'll need to make sure you have enough to enjoy your new life in Oregon City. Paying for a guide after you've spent so much could be a waste.

"We could try to make it down the river ourselves," you say. "We can go very slowly. Communicate about rocks up ahead."

Pa and Ma agree that you should save as much money as possible.

You build two rafts and start off down the river, leaving your wagons behind. Pa and the other men drive the livestock along the bank of the river. You didn't anticipate how strong this river's current would be, or how many small rapids would cause your rafts to tip. One strong dip into a rocky patch sends your rafts tipping over completely. You and the others are dragged under the strong currents.

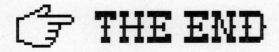 **THE END**

You need more food, but you've just lost one ox to exhaustion. Your team wouldn't make it if you sold off two more.

"We can sell off things we don't need." You scrape what few valuables you have left and try to sell them, but no one needs them here at the station.

"Sorry, folks," says the station manager. "We need useful supplies. Blankets, clothing, shoes."

You and your parents exchange frustrated glances.

"But we need these supplies to get to Oregon City." Ma holds onto a blanket. "We can't sell these!"

The man shrugs. "Sorry, ma'am. Nothing I can do."

You take your parents aside. "What if we went back to The Dalles?"

Pa sighs. "Go back the way we came?"

"We can't afford to pay the toll and buy more food, Pa. What if we try to meet up with the other two wagons at the river?"

You've come this far, but it wouldn't make much sense to keep going if you can't afford anything in

Oregon City. Coming to the Barlow Gate was a mistake.

"All right," says Pa. "Let's try it. We don't have much of a choice."

You wave goodbye to the Masons, who continue along the Barlow Road. The Whittakers agree to go back with you, as they can't afford to pay the toll and buy supplies either.

You reach the Columbia River. The current is strong and the water is rushing by at a high level. It's been raining and snowing in the area. Should you try to raft down the river now or wait to see if the other wagons show up first?

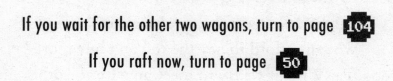

If you wait for the other two wagons, turn to page **104**

If you raft now, turn to page **50**

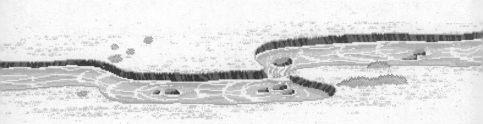

You remind Pa that he has agreed to be a doctor in Oregon City and that it's not a good idea to split up the wagon train.

"It's better if we keep going to Oregon City, Mr. Whittaker," you say. "I've been hearing from some traders and soldiers in the fort that the Gold Rush might be over."

Mr. Whittaker frowns. "Have you? I suppose I'll have to ask around, then."

"That might be a smart idea." Pa nods. "Let us know your decision by the end of the day, but we'd be sorry to see you go."

Mr. Whittaker returns within the next few hours, his head hung low. "I think you were right." He holds his hat in his hands. "I ran into a family on their way back from California. They're heading back East. Looks like whatever gold was in California seems to have been swept up in the Rush."

"Does that mean you and the O'Neils are staying

with our wagon train?" Ma wipes her hands on her apron.

The carpenter nods. "That we are."

"In that case, Mr. Whittaker. I think you and your family need to come join us for some slices of my famous apple pie." Ma reaches for the skillet.

You're so relieved the Whittakers and O'Neils aren't leaving for California. That night, you, Matthew, and Annie play games around the campfire. You tell one another what you look forward to the most in Oregon City.

"Finally having our own brand-new farmhouse," Annie says. "With more horses than we can count!"

"Having more food than I can stomach." Matthew pats his belly. "All the chicken and potatoes in the world."

You laugh. "You just had two slices of pie. You can't still be hungry."

"I'm always hungry."

The next morning, Ma gets some last-minute supplies at the small store in the fort, including another pair of shoes for each of you. "You'll need them for the mountains ahead. And we should probably get a few more blankets—just not from a swindler!"

You both grin at the reminder of that "trader" in Big Springs.

"Excuse me." A uniformed man approaches you. "I couldn't help but overhear. If you're going farther on the Trail, there's a patch of alkaline springs up ahead. Bad drinking water. There have been some bad bouts of cholera in the area."

"Thank you," you say. "We'll be sure to be careful."

You leave Fort Hall and eventually continue on through Fort Boise, the last fort before you get into mountain territory. You can't believe you've made it this far with your entire wagon train intact! You've stuck together, and that is the most important thing out here in the West.

One morning, you come across a lone wagon headed in the opposite direction. It's a young man with his head hung low, at the reins of four very sad-looking oxen. When he sees you, he waves wildly.

Pa pulls the reins and stops. The other five wagons pause in line after him.

"Hello, there!" Pa calls. "What seems to be the trouble?"

"Sir, I am in desperate need of your help," the young man says. "I had been on the Trail with my family, but they fell ill with cholera not even two days ago. I am the only one left. I've been wandering around for miles. I'm not sure where I am anymore. I haven't slept in hours. Can you help me?"

Pa casts an uneasy look to you and Ma. Of course, as a doctor, he wants to help. As captain, he wants to ensure the safety of the wagon train.

"How can we help?" Pa asks kindly.

"Would you be able to help me get back to Fort

Boise? I need to properly bury my parents." The young man points to the back of his wagon.

You left Fort Boise about a day ago, and you're already into the heart of the Blue Mountains. You'd lose too much time going back. Pa knows he has a responsibility to help those in need.

"What do you think?" he murmurs to you and Ma. "Should we help escort him back to the fort?"

You're not sure what to do. You know Pa should help the poor young man, but you also have to think about your own wagon train.

If you try to offer another kind of support, turn to page **135**

If you help the young man get to Fort Boise,
turn to page **39**

You choose to run for the gun instead of waking Pa. He'll be awake in a minute, anyway. King George and George Washington are already starting to bark and howl at the surrounding predators.

You rush to load the gun, but your fingers are sweating and shaky. You lift the gun toward the nearby yapping sounds of the coyotes, heaving it to your shoulder—

BANG!

The gun accidentally misfires. It blinds you with a puff of smoke and sends you tumbling back to the ground. Your ears ring, and all you can feel is pain. Your wagon train trek ends here.

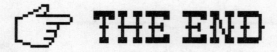 **THE END**

You need to help this poor young man in some way, but if you escort him back to Fort Boise, you will lose too much time. Your wagon train may decide to go on without you.

"What if we help him bury his family here?" you suggest to Pa and Ma. "And give him a map and some of our food and supplies?"

"Of course we can." Ma's eyes soften. "The poor boy has lost everything. The least we can do is give him food and blankets if he needs them."

"We'll just need to be careful," says Pa. "Cholera spreads easily."

He offers to help the young man bury his family and supply him with whatever he needs to return to Fort Boise. "Unfortunately, we will not be able to accompany you there personally. But we can provide a map and directions, should you need them."

The man is grateful for the help. Together, Pa, Mr. Whittaker, and Mr. O'Neil dig graves for the young man's parents. A small funeral service is held.

Ma hands the young man a thick blanket and

a small supply of flour, cornmeal, and well-packed bacon.

"Thank you for your help." He puts his hands together. "It all happened so fast. One minute we were camped by some pleasant streams near a valley, and the next day, my parents were violently ill—shakes, fever, and worse. They were both dead before I could blink."

"Your wagon was alone?" Pa's eyes widen.

The young man nods. "We had others with us, but some split off to take the Santa Fe Trail, and others . . . didn't make it. Trampled by their own wagons. Dysentery. My family was the last wagon left. And now there's no way I'll make it to Oregon City."

You feel bad for him. You're even more relieved that your entire wagon train has made it this far on the Trail.

You part ways with the stranger the next day and continue on through the Blue Mountains. You reach a narrow valley that dips down into a crystal-blue river. Trees line either side, but for the most part, the mountains are bare.

"Grande Ronde Valley." Pa raises his spectacles. "Down there. We're getting close to The Dalles."

You're grateful for a valley after all the rugged terrain you've crossed. You still have a lot of difficult land to cover.

Your family leads the wagon train into the valley, where you unhitch the oxen to let them graze on grass. King George and George Washington race to herd the livestock near the wagons. Trixie has to be nudged back to camp not once but twice before nightfall.

Your wagons corral for the night. Sitting around the campfire, you chew on rabbit Pa hunted earlier. You hear yaps and howls echoing in the hills.

"Coyotes." Pa frowns. "They're bold in these mountains."

"We need to make sure we keep a close eye on the stock tonight," Ma warns. "Mrs. Whittaker just told me they already lost one sheep they bought at Fort Boise to coyotes this afternoon. The Masons almost lost their cow. These coyotes are smart and fearless."

You pat Trixie's soft nose. You need to make sure she's well tied up for the night. If she wanders off, she'll be coyote bait.

Howling and yapping surround your wagon corral the whole night. The noises get closer to your

tent. You hear rustling in the trees and soft, padded feet scurrying about. Trixie lets out a low moo. Then you hear King George and George Washington let out deep growls.

The coyotes are trying to get to your animals!

You scramble out of your tent, blinking into the darkness. Pa's gun is just inside the wagon. He's shown you how to load it, although you've never actually fired a gun. Should you hurry to load it yourself or wake your parents instead?

If you load the gun yourself, turn to page **134**

If you wake your parents, turn to page **150**

The oxen are exhausted, but staying put is asking for trouble. Those men were well armed. Nearly everyone in your wagon train knows how to hunt, but not how to fight.

Despite your aching feet and body screaming for rest, you encourage Pa to tell the rest of the wagon train to keep moving. You know that settling down and setting up a series of campfires could encourage the fur traders to return.

When Pa and Ma inform the others of your plan, several families stare at you in disbelief.

"Excuse me, Doctor, but are you mad?" Mr. Whittaker's jaw drops. "We've been traveling all day. We can barely keep our own heads up, much less ask our oxen to keep going. They'll die of sheer exhaustion in the next hour."

"Those men have already moved on." Mrs. Whittaker fixes her bonnet. "They said they were trappers. They weren't interested in a wagon train. If they'd wanted to rob us, they could've done it right then and there, don't you think?"

You don't agree, but when the other families refuse to move on, Pa isn't sure what to do.

"We really shouldn't split up the wagon train," he tries to persuade them. "It's best if we stay together."

Mr. Whittaker shakes his head. "I'm sorry, Doctor. We're not moving."

Pa looks at Ma.

"I don't think we should stay," she murmurs. "Who knows what those men might do if they return?"

"Ma's right," you say, terrified.

Pa finally agrees. "All right. We'll keep moving and hope we reach Big Springs before it gets completely dark."

You sadly wave goodbye to Annie and Matthew as your wagon rolls away into the early evening hours.

You've hardly gotten more than a mile when you hear a low laugh in the trees.

"Well, well, what have we here? Seems like someone's a long way off from their wagon train, ain't it?"

You hear the click of a gun.

It's the fur trappers! They must have come back around to ambush any passing stragglers—like you.

Pa has to hand over all your money and any valuable supplies. None of you are hurt, but you have nothing left. Your dreams of opportunity in Oregon City have gone up in puffs of smoke.

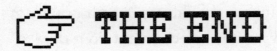 **THE END**

You think of your patchwork canvas and the rest of the damage the storm has done to your wagon train. You can't risk getting caught in another storm.

"Maybe by the time the wagons are caulked, the river will have gone down," you say hopefully.

"Hmm." Pa wipes his spectacles. "I'm just afraid of that river doing more damage than we can handle. But . . . if Mr. Mason is already in need of more supplies, it's our duty as leaders to make sure he's taken care of. We need to ensure everyone's safety and well-being above all else."

You nod. Everyone in the wagon train elected your family to be the captains—you can't let people down.

"That settles it." Pa turns back to Mr. Mason and Mr. Whittaker. "We'll confirm with the other families, but if they agree, we'll caulk the wagons carefully and ford the river as soon as everyone's ready."

Mr. Whittaker still doesn't look too pleased with the idea. "Are you sure about this, Doctor?"

Pa nods reluctantly. "We need to make it to Big Springs as soon as possible."

"Quite so, quite so." Mr. Mason sighs with relief. "Thank you, Doctor."

You all return to the wagon corral, where Pa gathers the other families to confer about the decision.

The other families aren't on board with the idea. They will wait. You, the Masons, and the Whittakers will go on to cross the river now.

After caulking the wagons, you help Pa control the oxen and carefully wade across the river. At its deepest, the river is nearly above your head. The oxen rear and tug at their ropes in the raging current.

The ropes snap, and two of your oxen are carried

away by the river. You let out a cry, but it's useless. They're gone.

"Just keep going!" Pa shouts.

The riverbed beneath you is murky and thick. Mud seeps into your shoes.  One shoe is pulled off as you struggle to cross to the other side.

"No!" You hear a wail from Mr. Mason, and a loud *crack!*

You glance back to see his second wagon tipping over in the current. Supplies and valuables float down the river.

By the time the four wagons cross, you've lost several hundred pounds of food, several sets of clothing, and multiple boxes of ammunition. Two of your six oxen are gone.

"We should have waited." Mr. Whittaker's eyes flash. He's lost his only set of carpentry tools.

You swallow hard. You feel as though this is all your fault.

Pa frowns. "It's too late to lay blame now. We have to keep going."

Before Big Springs comes the difficult terrain of an enormous hill called Hogback Ridge—or more infamously, Devil's Backbone. Crossing this steep terrain costs you more time than you anticipated. Your exhausted team of oxen barely makes it up the hill.

Big Springs isn't exactly what its name implies. It's hardly more than a church, a small general store, and a few small houses in the town circle.

You need supplies and new oxen, but you don't have much left to trade. Should you stock up on food or try to trade for two new oxen?

If you stock up on food, turn to page **36**

If you trade for new oxen, turn to page **57**

The rest of the wagon train is worried about their own families' proximity to the young man. And while Pa does have medicine, the young man will likely have more of a chance of surviving if he's in a proper bed at the fort.

"Maybe they'll have more medicine, too, Pa," you reason.

"I'm sure they're better equipped to deal with this than we are, out here on the Trail," Ma agrees. "Let's go back. It's not terribly far."

You tell the other families your plan. The Whittakers agree to stay and wait for you, but the two other families decide to follow the Masons and go on without you. You're disappointed that your whole wagon train won't wait for you, but there's nothing you can do about it. You can only hope that you'll eventually be reunited. Then, you start to wonder if this was the best decision to make as the wagon-train captains. Splitting up your wagon train is never a good idea.

You understand why Pa has to make this difficult choice. Being a doctor can often require sacrifice, even if it means separating your wagon train.

You and your parents place the sick stranger in the back of your wagon and start off for Fort Boise. He becomes progressively worse, despite your family's best efforts. By the time you reach Fort Boise, he's passed away. You sadly bury him with the help of some soldiers at the fort. You start back on the Trail, hoping you can catch up with the others before it's too late. Fur trappers at the fort had just come from Flagstaff Hill and mentioned how snowstorms can come on without warning and completely decimate a wagon train.

You haven't been traveling for more than half a day when the clouds gather and snow falls in thick blots from the sky. Before you know it, your wagon is

stuck in mud and wet snow. Without help from your
fellow wagon-train families or a way to get back to
the fort, you and your family are soon swallowed up
in the snowstorm, never to be heard from again.

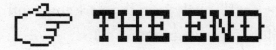 **THE END**

You slip out of your tent and rush across to your parents' tent.

"Pa, wake up!" You pull off his blanket. "Coyotes nearby!"

Pa races to the wagon. He loads his gun quickly and orders you to rekindle the fire. "The fire will keep them away!" He starts shouting at the coyotes lingering around the corral. "Hey, get away!"

Your dogs growl angrily into the darkness, and the other families come running to help.

You throw some buffalo chips onto the dying embers of the giant campfire and carefully blow on the ashes. The fire roars to life. After a tense standoff, Pa and the others chase the coyotes off into the hills.

Pa comes to warm his hands near the fire. "Good thing you woke me. They almost had Trixie."

You shiver. It's only gotten colder here in the mountains. Even in the darkness, you see the

faint spots of snow falling around the campfire.
You remember people at Fort Boise telling you that
snowstorms and avalanches are common disasters that
can strike at any time in the Blue Mountains. You
hope that doesn't happen to your wagon train.

The next morning, you wake up still exhausted
from the danger of the night before. Your feet feel
especially heavy and drag through the freshly fallen
snow. Even the oxen are slower than usual, barely
making it up the slushy mountains.

Your wagon starts to slip backwards down the
hill. Ma lets out a frightened shout, holding tightly to
the reins. Pa attempts to calm the oxen, whose hooves
slip in the muck. You rush to grab the other side of
the yoke. Eventually you both manage to stop the
oxen and reroute their path up the mountain.

When you finally reach the top, you look down
and discover that some supplies have fallen out in the
chaos and slid down the hillside. It's too dangerous to
retrieve anything in the steep slush.

Your wagon isn't the only one to lose supplies.
One of the Masons' wagons loses an ox, and Mr.

O'Neil breaks an arm wrangling his wagon up the mountain. Pa has to set Mr. O'Neil's arm in a makeshift sling.

It will be a miracle if everyone in your wagon train makes it to Oregon City. So far, you've lost only animals and supplies. But there are still treacherous roads and rivers ahead.

That evening, two Cayuse men named Ya'ka and I'mes pass through your campsite. Ya'ka is injured from fighting off a wild mountain lynx. Pa treats his injuries. In thanks, the men offer helpful information.

"Ya'ka and I'mes told us there's bad weather near The Dalles." Pa takes a seat. The men have already departed into the mountains. "The river can be high this time of year—and the storm has only made it

worse. Let's rest for a day or two, especially with Mr. O'Neil's arm."

Mr. O'Neil grimaces. "Won't be easy makin' it the rest of the way, Doc. That's for sure."

"What if we take the Barlow Road instead?" Mrs. Mason steps in. "We've lost so much already in these mountains—time . . . supplies. Who knows how much we'll lose if we try to raft down the Columbia River?"

"Don't think I can afford the toll." Mr. Whittaker pats his pocket. "That last stop at Fort Boise set me back more than I wanted. I still need to buy new supplies in Oregon City."

Mr. O'Neil agrees, as does your pa.

"What if we trap rabbits and hunt around here?"

you say. "That way the oxen—and Mr. O'Neil—can rest for a bit."

"The Barlow Road isn't that far from here," Mr. Mason argues. "We can make it."

Pa and Ma look at each other, uncertain. You know Mr. O'Neil isn't in good shape to travel right now. But you do need supplies. What should you do?

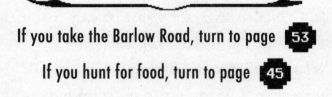

If you take the Barlow Road, turn to page **53**

If you hunt for food, turn to page **45**

You hesitate, but Pa is right. Nervous oxen are dangerous oxen. They could get scared and run off, trampling someone—including you! It'll be dark in a couple of hours too. If the oxen are scared now and run off, it'll be a disaster trying to find them in the dying sunlight.

"Yes, Pa." You sigh, and watch Annie and Matthew running away toward the river. You head back to help Pa and Ma unhitch the oxen.

You hear Mrs. Whittaker calling for her children to return to their wagon. "Annie and Matthew—it's not safe by the river!" You see little William crawling after her. "Get back here, both of you!"

The Whittaker siblings reluctantly return, their heads hung low. Still, you grin at them as they pass. They smile in return. You know you've just made some fast friends.

As night falls on your camp, thick clouds cover the stars, and thunder rolls across the plains, rustling

and whistling through the trees. Lightning flashes in thick purple streaks, and you jump under your blanket. Fear tugs at your heart. A spring storm is the last thing you want before crossing a difficult river. You lie in your tent as the wind howls and rain lashes down, followed by thundering balls of hail. You sleep very little.

The next morning, you wake up to discover that your wagon's canvas top has been damaged in the storm. A bag of flour has been torn open and spilled all over the ground.

"We needed this flour." Ma sighs. "We'll just have to stock up in Big Springs."

"At least Mr. Whittaker can help repair our wagon." You look at the enormous hole.

"Oh, no," Ma says dryly. "You can help me with that. Come on. We should have a spare piece of cloth somewhere."

Together you stitch the canvas back together. It's *almost* as good as new!

"It'll have to do," says Ma. "Hopefully we won't encounter another storm like that again."

You agree, remembering how frightened you were last night.

After helping with the morning chores, you follow Pa down toward the river, where he talks with Mr. Whittaker and the banker, Mr. Mason. The riverbank is steeper than you expected: a mixture of thick, squishy mud and limestone. The river rushes below.

"It's too high," says Mr. Whittaker grimly. "I was asking around the junction, and this riverbed is exceptionally thick and muddy, making it difficult for wagons to cross. If we tried to ford it, we'd be taking a risk. We should caulk the wagons to seal them so they can float. Then, we'll tow them across and up the other bank. Once the river settles down, that is."

"Caulk the wagons?" Mr. Mason shifts his weight. "And how long will *that* take, may I ask?"

Pa crosses his arms. "The storm last night was

bad. You think crossing the river as high as it is now is a good idea, Mr. Mason?"

Mr. Mason pauses to wipe his brow. "Well, fine. Let's hurry up and do what we need to do. No time to lose."

Mr. Whittaker shakes his head. "No. Not until the river is lower. We'd never make it across. We should wait at least a day."

"We can't afford to lose any more time!" Mr. Mason turns red. "We have to get to Big Springs to restock."

You exchange bewildered glances with Pa and Mr. Whittaker.

"You have not one, but *two* wagons for your family, Mr. Mason," says Mr. Whittaker. "You can't be running out of supplies already. Not when we only left Independence a few days ago. You have no children. You and your wife should have plenty of room for food and other necessities."

"Most of what is in our wagons just so happens to be important valuables!" Mr. Mason bellows. "We didn't have room! And this storm damaged one of our

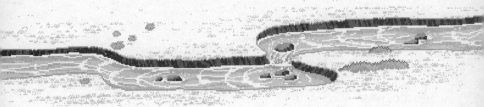

wagons nearly beyond repair. It'll be a miracle if it makes it to Big Springs."

"Gentlemen, please," Pa says. He takes you aside. "What do you think? *We* may need supplies soon too."

What should you do?

If you ford the river soon, turn to page **143**

If you wait until the river is lower, turn to page **111**

You stare down at your mismatched feet. "I'd like to stop at Fort Vancouver, Pa."

Ma looks at your feet. "I didn't even realize— where did your shoe go?"

"The river wanted it more than I did."

Pa shakes his head. "You can get sick very quickly without shoes. Especially in this cold, rainy weather."

Ma digs around in one of your satchels until she finds a thick hunting knife, a piece of buckskin, and a sewing kit. She cuts off a strip of the buckskin and wraps the piece around your foot. "At least we can try to wrap it up in something until we can get you a new pair." She sews your foot into the buckskin.

Mr. Whittaker clears his throat. "Doc, not to interrupt, but none of us has much money left. You really think stopping at Fort Vancouver's the best idea when we're so close to Oregon City?"

Pa fumbles with his pocket knife. "It's a group decision. I'd like to see if I can get a better splint for Mr. O'Neil. It's still a good stretch downriver to Oregon City . . . A short respite would do us good."

The group is silent for a moment around the campfire.

Finally, Mrs. Mason says, "Well, Dr. Howard, you've led us this far, and we've all survived, which is more than most wagon trains can say. So I think I can speak for the group that we'll agree with whatever decision you make."

Everyone else nods eagerly.

Pa swallows, and you see tears in his eyes. He wipes off his spectacles and clears his throat. "I couldn't have done it without my family." He smiles at you and Ma. "But thank you, everyone. We've been honored to be your wagon-train captains this far. We'll make it the rest of the way together, we will."

"To Fort Vancouver, then!" Mr. Whittaker raises his coffee cup.

You wish you didn't have to get back on the

raft, but knowing that you'll stop only shortly ahead makes the next several miles downriver much easier. The weather has also gotten better. It's finally stopped raining, and the sun is beginning to peek through the clouds.

When you reach Fort Vancouver, you dock your rafts and decide to take turns watching the supplies while everyone gets what they need. The fort is a British fur-trading post filled with soldiers, Native Americans from all different Nations, and hordes of other pioneers on their way to Oregon City.

It's much more crowded than you anticipated, but you manage to squeeze through the masses of people to stop and trade. You come across a Nez Perce woman, who introduces herself as Táyam, selling beautiful leather moccasins—the perfect size for your feet. After you and Ma pay and thank Táyam, you slip them on and breathe a sigh of relief, wiggling your toes. You've never had shoes this comfortable before in your life!

Annie and Matthew are also eager to get off the raft and explore.

Matthew stares down at your moccasins, wide-eyed. "Those look so nice. Almost as nice as mine." He stares down at his heavily patched-up shoes with a rueful grin.

The three of you laugh.

"I'm sure you can get some new shoes when you get to Oregon City," you say.

He just shrugs. "I just really want some candy."

Before you leave Fort Vancouver, you share a meal with your family at the local tavern with the money you saved by avoiding the Barlow Toll Road. You haven't had a nice steak with potatoes or such a big piece of pie in *months*. Now you can hardly wait to get to Oregon City and have meals like this almost every day!

When you leave Fort Vancouver the next morning, you thank your invaluable guide Ow-hi and continue on your rafts down the much smaller Willamette River. On either side is beautiful, lush green country. You're surprised, and pleased, to finally

see columns of smoke rising from small farmhouses dotting the landscape.

You can hardly believe it when you see the busy port of Oregon City. You haven't seen a real town or city this big since leaving Independence. You want to pinch yourself, you're so excited. But what's more incredible is that your entire wagon train has made it here. There have been damaged and lost supplies—even broken bones—but considering all the many dangers you've faced on the Oregon Trail, it's a wonder that everyone in your wagon train is alive.

Everyone in your group lets out a sigh of relief and a cheer of joy when you finally get into Oregon City. Some families depart right away, looking to claim land and settle their livestock. You and the

Whittakers remain in town to board your oxen temporarily while you find something to eat and rest at a nearby inn.

"Guess what?" Annie skips excitedly down the road alongside you. "Ma just told me we'll be nearby! Our pa is going to be helping to build a new courthouse right next to your pa's practice!"

You're all joyful and relieved, knowing you'll have one another as good friends in this new and unfamiliar city. Now more than ever, you're excited to explore your new surroundings—and with the Whittaker siblings around, everything will be that much more adventurous and fun.

You can't wait to start your new life in Oregon City. You know that all your months on the Oregon Trail have been worth it for this. You've successfully led a full wagon train and completed your long journey West—together.

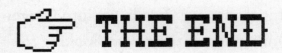 **THE END**

Oregon City
SEPTEMBER 19, 1855

GUIDE
to the Trail

You are about to embark on an incredible journey as one of the 400,000 adventurous and daring pioneers who are trekking West between 1841 and 1870. You will be traveling roughly 2,000 miles (3,200 kilometers) along the Oregon Trail with everything you own tightly packed into a covered wagon. There will be dangers and adventures that you've never experienced before.

What do you have to look forward to when you get out West?

- A square mile of land for your family on which to build a house
- New opportunities to start a new life away from crowded cities
- Fertile land and plenty of rain for farming crops

PACK YOUR WAGON

Your ten-foot-long covered wagon will carry your supplies for your new life in the Oregon Territory. There won't be room to ride in it, so you'll have to walk. Don't forget to buy six healthy oxen to pull your wagon!

You will need two hundred pounds of food per person, mainly flour, bacon, sugar, cornmeal, fat, beans, rice, vinegar, baking soda, and citric acid. Pack your essential building, farming, and wagon-repair tools and camping gear such as a tent, bedding, kitchen utensils, matches, rope, and candles.

Make sure you bring extra sets of thick, woolen clothing for the colder mountainous regions. Take buckskin and sewing materials for repairing shoes. Remember: choose how you spend your money wisely. You don't want to reach Oregon City completely broke!

JOIN A WAGON TRAIN

Pioneers will join wagon "trains," which are groups of wagons traveling together. Smaller groups are more manageable than large ones, but if you're traveling with many wagons, be sure to keep everyone together at all costs. The advantages of larger wagon trains

include safety in numbers, helping one another with skills, and hunting in packs. There are many dangers on the Trail, so a larger wagon train will likely mean better chances of survival and success.

Keep on the lookout for bad weather, rest when needed, and listen to your fellow pioneers.

Your days will start as early as four in the morning, with breakfast, chores, and loading your wagon. A bugle at seven means it's time to start the day's journey. The wagon train will roll along until six p.m., except for an hour's lunch and rest time, which is called "nooning."

At the end of the day, you will unload your wagon, set up camp, take care of your livestock, and cook dinner. If you can't find firewood, you can burn dried patties of buffalo dung called "buffalo chips." Sometimes you play games or tell stories around the campfire.

DANGERS!

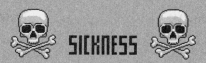

SICKNESS

Cholera and dysentery are deadly diseases that can kill a person within a day. Highly contagious and caught by drinking unclean water or eating uncooked food, cholera was the main cause of death on the Trail. Cook your food thoroughly and boil drinking water.

DISHONEST PEOPLE

The Trail is riddled with bandits and deceptive traders. Be sure to always be on your guard and ask around before purchasing wares.

BAD WEATHER

Sudden thunderstorms, snowstorms, avalanches, and bad weather can damage wagons, destroy food and livestock, and result in sickness and even death if you're not prepared.

SEPARATION

Splitting up your wagon train is rarely a good idea. Stay together! There is safety in numbers. You need support and community on this dangerous Trail.

CROSSING RIVERS

Crossing any river is difficult for a heavy wagon filled with supplies and valuables. Some riverbeds can be thick and muddy, making it easy for the wagon wheels to sink in deep and get stuck. Make sure the river is low if you're going to ford it, and get help navigating when you can.

ANIMALS

Predators such as snakes and coyotes can easily kill and hurt your livestock. Make loud noises and get help if you hear howling nearby. Be wary of tall prairie grasses, where snakes can easily hide.

☞ FINDING YOUR WAY

In 1855, once you leave Independence, Missouri, you are striking out into the great open wilderness. There are no roads, no inns, and no towns. The United States comprises thirty-one states and busy cities and towns back East. But out West, you'll have to cross territories and Native American lands by using a compass, consulting a map of the Oregon Trail (such as the one at the front of the book on pages 4 and 5), and looking for famous landmarks, listed below.

At settlements and forts along the way, trail guides and friendly locals can provide good advice.

Look for these landmarks between Missouri and Oregon City

DISTANCE FROM INDEPENDENCE, MISSOURI:

GARDNER JUNCTION: 42 miles (68 km)

BIG SPRINGS: 65 miles (105 km)

FORT HALL: 1,217 miles (1,959 km)

THE DALLES: 1,732 miles (2,787 km)

The Oregon Trail™

LIVE the Adventure!

Do you have what it takes to make it all the way to Oregon City?

Look straight into the face of danger and dysentery.

Read all the books in this new choose-your-own-trail series!

The Oregon Trail

THE RACE TO CHIMNEY ROCK

More than 20 possible endings!

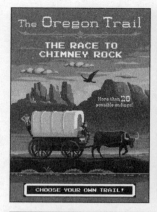

CHOOSE YOUR OWN TRAIL!

The Oregon Trail

DANGER AT THE HAUNTED GATE

More than 20 possible endings!

CHOOSE YOUR OWN TRAIL!

The Oregon Trail

THE SEARCH FOR SNAKE RIVER

More than 20 possible endings!

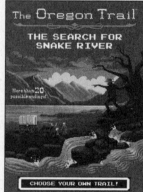

CHOOSE YOUR OWN TRAIL!

The Oregon Trail

THE ROAD TO OREGON CITY

More than 20 possible endings!

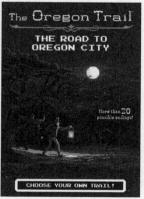

CHOOSE YOUR OWN TRAIL!

The Oregon Trail

THE WAGON TRAIN TREK

More than 20 possible endings!

CHOOSE YOUR OWN TRAIL!

The Oregon Trail

ALONE IN THE WILD

More than 20 possible endings!

CHOOSE YOUR OWN TRAIL!